Two Turtle Doves

Twelve Days of Christmas

Emily E K Murdoch

ARE YOU SIGNED UP FOR DRAGONBLADE'S BLOG?

You'll get the latest news and information on exclusive giveaways, exclusive excerpts, coming releases, sales, free books, cover reveals and more.

Check out our complete list of authors, too!

No spam, no junk. That's a promise!

Sign Up Here

www.dragonbladepublishing.com

Dearest Reader;

Thank you for your support of a small press. At Dragonblade Publishing, we strive to bring you the highest quality Historical Romance from some of the best authors in the business. Without your support, there is no 'us', so we sincerely hope you adore these stories and find some new favorite authors along the way.

Happy Reading!

CEO, Dragonblade Publishing

Additional Dragonblade books by Author Emily E K Murdoch

Twelve Days of Christmas
Twelve Drummers Drumming
Eleven Pipers Piping
Ten Lords a Leaping
Nine Ladies Dancing
Eight Maids a Milking
Seven Swans a Swimming
Six Geese a Laying
Five Gold Rings
Four Calling Birds
Three French Hens
Two Turtle Doves
A Partridge in a Pear Tree

The De Petras Saga
The Misplaced Husband (Book 1)
The Impoverished Dowry (Book 2)
The Contrary Debutante (Book 3)
The Determined Mistress (Book 4)
The Convenient Engagement (Book 5)

The Governess Bureau Series
A Governess of Great Talents (Book 1)
A Governess of Discretion (Book 2)
A Governess of Many Languages (Book 3)
A Governess of Prodigious Skill (Book 4)
A Governess of Unusual Experience (Book 5)
A Governess of Wise Years (Book 6)
A Governess of No Fear (Novella)

Never The Bride Series

Always the Bridesmaid (Book 1)
Always the Chaperone (Book 2)
Always the Courtesan (Book 3)
Always the Best Friend (Book 4)
Always the Wallflower (Book 5)
Always the Bluestocking (Book 6)
Always the Rival (Book 7)
Always the Matchmaker (Book 8)
Always the Widow (Book 9)
Always the Rebel (Book 10)
Always the Mistress (Book 11)
Always the Second Choice (Book 12)
Always the Mistletoe (Novella)
Always the Reverend (Novella)

The Lyon's Den Series
Always the Lyon Tamer

Pirates of Britannia Series
Always the High Seas

De Wolfe Pack: The Series
Whirlwind with a Wolfe

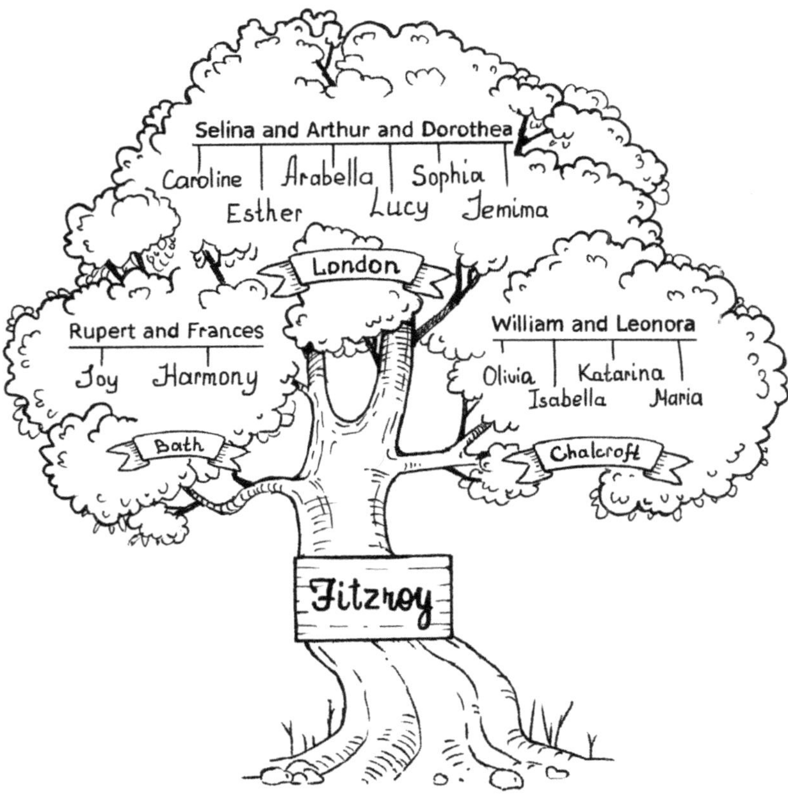

Selina and Arthur and Dorothea
Caroline
Arabella
Sophia
Esther
Lucy
Jemima
London
Rupert and Frances
Joy
Harmony
William and Leonora
Olivia
Katarina
Isabella
Maria
Bath
Chalcroft
Fitzroy

CHAPTER ONE

"—AND THE WAY he chews on my gowns, Mama, I simply cannot tell you! There must be a way to stop him doing such a thing; it is most provoking—"

"Yes, I know, most infuriating. Have you tried putting a little vinegar on your hems? I always find—"

"Mama! I cannot go around smelling of vinegar!"

Joy Fitzroy silently turned a page in her book and thanked the stars she was not required to contribute to such a dull conversation.

Really! Her sister Harmony and their mother may as well be talking about a puppy who was misbehaving, rather than her nephew!

"That is always the way with children—they learn precisely what one does not like, then proceed to do precisely that," said Frances wisely, nodding her head over a cup of tea.

Harmony sighed on the sofa beside her. "I knew children were difficult, but this…"

Joy turned another page of her book. She was not actually reading it; it was a novel she had read so many times she could almost recite the darn thing.

No, as an interesting book it was useless—but as a shield from having to participate in the conversation, it was golden. Everyone knew not to interrupt Joy when she was reading.

"But, of course, the joy of having a child surmounts all." Harmony smiled prettily, glancing at her sister.

Joy looked down immediately, cursing her decision to look up at that moment. Her cheeks warmed slightly, as though she had been caught. Which was ridiculous, of course. This was her home, wasn't it?

Well, her parents' home. But she had grown up here, lived here as a child, as a young lady coming out into Society, and now...

Joy sighed heavily as she turned a page in the awkward silence of the room. Now she had to sit here and listen to her younger sister prattle on about the delights and challenges of having a husband and children while she...

She was alone.

"I have heard whispers from your cousins in London—they believe a wedding is in order!"

Joy could not help it. Her curiosity overcame her and she looked up again. Frances, her mother, was beaming at Harmony, who clapped her hands in excitement.

"Sophia? Well of course it's Sophia. I do not know why I asked—she is the last unmarried London Fitzroy, of course!"

A painful twist in her stomach forced Joy to return her gaze to the page before her; words swam in and out of her vision.

She was not going to let it affect her. She wasn't. She had nerves of steel—had to, living in Bath, seeing countless chits from the country come here, dance three dull dances with a dull gentleman, and receive an offer of marriage. While she...

Joy swallowed. She was not going to think it.

...was left behind.

Blast.

"And, of course, now Maria's had her second child, it will be busy at Chalcroft this Christmas," added Harmony. "Goodness, so many grandchildren! I wonder how Aunt Leonora can manage them all."

"Yes, I am quite happy with my little Rufus," their mother

said fondly. "Though I would not say no to any further... I mean... Ahem."

Joy did not need to look up to know both her mother and sister had looked over at her, flushed, then looked away.

Why had they not permitted her to leave when Harmony arrived for her visit? She had known full well what the topics of conversation would be, and all were tedious to her mind.

Babies, music, children, matrimony, the best lace one could find outside of London.

Not exactly the scintillating chatter she hoped for.

A curl of guilt wrapped itself around her heart, one Joy attempted to push away.

That is the trouble, isn't it? a dark voice within her whispered. *You say you do not like these topics, but that is only because you are...*

I am not jealous, Joy told herself firmly. Not in the slightest.

It was a lie, of course. There was only so long one could cope with being the Fitzroy that was left behind. All her cousins, her sister: they had paraded along with their lives, marrying, having children—all except Jemima, and no one ever spoke about that.

And Isabella, of course, one of the Chalcroft cousins. Somehow everyone always forgot about Isabella.

But still. Joy could not help but feel most provoked by the continuous focus on babies. What about art, and nature, and science? What about the politics of the day? Was no one interested in her opinions on those?

"Now, you simply must tell me when you hear of Sophia's wedding plans," continued Harmony. "Particularly any musical choices. I must know—"

"I do not believe they are likely to announce such a thing before the wedding, Harmony, and you know that as well as I." Their mother laughed good-naturedly. "Besides, there is no guarantee there will be a wedding! From what I have heard, the Viscount Dunbar..."

Joy sighed heavily. Viscount Dunbar. That sounded a prestigious name, and Sophia would become a viscountess. Little

Sophia, whom Joy had been forced to look after on one of their visits six years ago. Why, she had not even been out at that time!

And now, six years later, Sophia would be married and Joy would have to resign herself to the position of...

She shuddered. *Maiden aunt.*

"Do you not think it a splendid thing, Sophia getting married?"

And the worst of it all, Joy thought bitterly as she turned another page of the book she was not reading, was that everyone would expect her to be so happy about it. As though another marriage in the family was in no way pointing out just how left behind she had become.

As though there was nothing in her life to celebrate, so she could only celebrate others!

"Joy?"

Joy looked up hurriedly. Her sister and mother were looking expectant, as though she had been involved in the conversation then suddenly drifted away.

"I beg your pardon?" she said coldly.

Neither Frances nor Harmony took any notice of her tone. *No surprise there*, Joy thought with a wry smile. It was often easier for them to ignore her tone. She really had to work on being less sarcastic; it was enough to drive even the best suitors away.

If she'd ever had any, of course.

"I said, is it not a splendid thing, Sophia getting married?" repeated her mother.

Joy's cheeks flushed, and her sister hissed under her breath.

"Mama! You know we don't mention marriages to Joy!"

"We cannot tiptoe around it—people get married all the time!" said Frances.

Joy smiled weakly, swallowing down her bitterness, her pain, and sat in silence. She should have guessed. They were keeping such topics from her; that would explain why she was not informed of Esther's wedding until two days before they left for Kendal.

They had assumed, perhaps rightly, that the news would upset her.

Well, she would just have to prove them wrong, wouldn't she? Joy Fitzroy was not going to permit herself to build a reputation of being unable to talk on some topics merely because she was emotional.

Even if it was true.

"How pleasant for Sophia," Joy said briskly, as though the conversation was a cold sea dip, and if she just launched herself in, she would soon be out. "Have the banns been read?"

Harmony glanced at their mother. "Well, no, not as far as—"

"Then there is no marriage to celebrate, nor congratulate," cut in Joy, as calmly as she could. "When there is, I will be sure to congratulate Cousin Sophia. At the appropriate time."

"I do not believe it will be long," said Frances. "Why, in my last letter from Selina, she says Sophia and Viscount Dunbar have been seen dancing—"

"Oh, well, rush to fetch a vicar and start up the organ," said Joy with a laugh. "Dancing! In public! They'll have to marry now!"

Harmony's face fell, and she glanced at their mother with a beseeching look.

Joy swallowed. *Blast.* That was too harsh, wasn't it? It was always easier to tell once she had spoken and the words were out there, floating in the air, and she saw the reaction of others.

She had not meant to be cruel, but really. *Dancing? In public?* If the family had believed she was to marry everyone she danced with, she would have far too many husbands.

"I believe he has an ill reputation," said Harmony softly.

Joy rolled her eyes. "Does not every gentleman? I swear, other than your David, Harmony, I am yet to meet a gentleman who has not already bedded—"

"Joy!"

"Well!" Joy said defiantly, meeting her mother's gaze, then dropping it to her lap.

It did not appear to matter how old one became—one's mother was always able to silence you with a look.

"You know what I mean," she continued. "A gentleman does not lose his reputation, no matter what ill activities he indulges in, whereas a lady—"

"A lady never tells," said Harmony, with a strange flush on her cheeks.

Joy stared at her younger sister. *Now what did that mean?* Little Harmony—she should not call her that; Harmony was a married mother, after all—talking about such things? And so coyly?

A lady never tells, indeed. Just what would Harmony have to tell? Joy could not imagine her sister doing anything untoward, lest their parents discover it. Even now, after six years of marriage, she was here at least twice a week.

"That is just the way of Society," said their mother, as though she'd ended the conversation.

Joy scoffed. "The way of Society? You mean that is the way it is, and you see no reason to change it."

"Joy—"

"I think it ridiculous, that is all. The only people who are able to do what they like are widows and widowers," continued Joy recklessly. "They can bed whom they like with no—"

"Joy Fitzroy!"

The three ladies turned, and heat rushed to Joy's face as she saw her father standing in the doorway. He had an astonished look on his face and a pipe in his hand.

"I beg your pardon?" he said slowly.

Joy swallowed. It was all very well speaking her mind before her mother and sister—they were hardly likely to disagree with her...or tell her father. Rupert was not a cruel man. *If anything,* Joy thought wryly, *he's too soft on his daughters.* But there was a line.

"We were just discussing the latest novel, my dear."

Joy turned to look at her mother, who was smiling beneficently at her husband.

"Novel?" repeated Rupert.

"Yes," said Joy hastily, picking up the book she had carelessly laid aside. "Goodness, Papa, you would not believe the things that happen! First there is a ball—"

"Yes, yes, I am sure there is," said Rupert with a wave of his hand. "Just ensure you do not discuss such things in front of little Rufus. I do believe he picks up every word I say." He meandered off down the hall.

Joy breathed a sigh of relief—one echoed by her companions in the drawing room.

"You must be more careful, Joy," said Frances. "Who knows who might hear you!"

"You do not wish to risk your reputation, after all," Harmony added, shaking her head as though she was older rather than younger. "Why, when a woman has no reputation—"

"She doesn't have anything," said Joy dully.

It was all too aggravating. She was right, after all: a lady's reputation was delicate, precarious, always at risk, while a gentleman…why, he could attend gaming dens, brothels, seduce ladies, fight in duels—and he was considered the absolute picture of a refined member of Society!

It was so irritating, she could scream!

"Now, tell me about your thoughts for a governess," said her mother to Harmony, eyes bright. "I have heard terrible things about the Governess Bureau. We cannot go there—"

"Oh, Mama, you do not know the half of it! I heard from a friend in London, and she wrote to me with all the details. It was two years ago, and Miss Vivienne Clarke…"

The conversation began washing over Joy again, and she let it. What could she contribute to a debate about governesses, after all? It was not as though she had any knowledge of the profession, aside from the poor governess they had been allotted years ago.

Joy sighed and opened up the book in her lap, glancing down at its pages but not taking in a word. Was this what her life would be forever? A continuous discussion of baby names, weaning, governesses... It would not be long before Rufus would be entering Society himself, and then they would have to go through the entire rigmarole again with his marriage, his children...

Her jaw clenched. *It was unending.* Would she ever find herself a part of her own life that did not continuously point out just how left behind she was?

"And what about you, Joy?"

Joy jerked up, looking at her mother and sister, who were once again looking at her expectantly.

This is what happens, she told herself sternly, *when you do not pay attention. You look like a fool!*

"I said," said Harmony softly, with none of the irritation her sister would have had if she had been forced to repeat herself, "what are you hoping for this Christmas?"

Joy glanced at the window. Gentle snow was falling, as was to be expected. It was but two weeks before Christmas, and the entire family would be leaving soon for Chalcroft, the seat of the Fitzroys, just an hour's carriage ride away.

And she would be reunited with all her cousins, their husbands, their children...

"I suppose I just need a family to fall into my lap this Christmas," said Joy, half joking, half serious as she turned back to her sister. "Then I would fit in with the rest of the Fitzroys."

Harmony's face flushed scarlet. "Y-you cannot have a child fall into your lap!"

Too late, Joy recalled the difficulty her sister had endured in falling with child. Five long years of marriage before Rufus had appeared. *Blast.*

"I know that," Joy said, "I just meant—"

"That is not a pleasant thing to say to your sister," interrupted Frances.

"I know!"

Joy felt fraught, taut, beleaguered, her nerves tightened beyond endurance. Why did the entirety of their conversations have to be about matrimony, babies, what Society expected of a lady, anyway? Why did she always have to feel as though she was left behind, unable to contribute to conversations or to the family, merely because she had not wed?

She rose suddenly, dropping the book to the floor. "I think I will go for a walk."

Her stiff voice was matched by her mother's. "I believe that would be a good idea."

Joy's heart twisted. Once, just once, she wanted her mother to clasp her in her arms and say it did not matter that she was not married, that one's worth was entirely separate from one's ability to have children.

But no. It would be best if Joy went for a walk. Of course it would.

Without stopping to say goodbye to Harmony, Joy swept past both of them and grabbed her thick pelisse in the hall. She would need it, and her gloves, in the cold, wintry air.

Despite her precautions, freezing air filled her lungs as Joy stepped outside.

"Goodness!" she could not help but exclaim—the temperature was freezing. The streets were almost empty, as most people were wisely deciding to stay indoors rather than venture out into the icy air.

Joy stamped her feet, wondering whether it was better to just turn around and go back inside. She could always go upstairs to her bedchamber rather than face her sister again…

But no. She hardened her heart and stepped down the path to the pavement. She was a grown woman, far beyond the age where she could merely hide in her room whenever she upset anyone!

No. She would hide outside instead.

Sydney Gardens were not far from the Fitzroy home, and it was in that direction that Joy turned, passing very few people on the streets, all just as bundled up against the cold as she.

The drifting snow placed a beautiful patina of crisp white upon everything she passed, and Joy tried to take notice of how elegant the trees looked, and how the flowerbeds waited calmly for spring.

But it was no good. A tear prickled the corner of her eye, threatening to fall, then did so, cooling her face instantly and disappearing into frost.

This was going to be a difficult Christmas. Joy had known it the moment the Chalcroft invitation arrived. Another Christmas with all the Fitzroys together—all twelve cousins. That meant ten husbands—perhaps eleven, if Sophia truly was about to wed the Viscount Dunbar and procured a special license—and goodness knew how many children.

Joy had attempted to keep count, she really had, but with a sister and ten cousins, the odds were against her.

A bench was in one corner of the gardens, and she sat heavily upon it, ignoring the freezing sensation on her behind.

Another tear fell down her cheek. She was pathetic. Here she was, out in the freezing cold, all because she would not suffer the indignity of conversing about everyone and their sister who had married and had children.

What had she said?

"I suppose I just need a family to fall into my lap this Christmas. Then I would fit in with the rest of the Fitzroys."

But there was no chance she would ever fit into the Fitzroys, not really. Joy knew that. It was impossible, and the sooner she learned to accept that, the—

A child fell into her lap.

CHAPTER TWO

J OY BLINKED IN utter astonishment at the child in her lap.

What? Was she dreaming? Had she fallen asleep on the bench in Sydney Gardens, her previous words whirling around her mind so insistently that they had conjured up a literal child from her imagination?

But Joy could feel the weight of the girl in her lap, hear her giggles. This was no dream.

"Hello," said the girl conversationally as she looked up at Joy.

"H-hello," stammered Joy.

This was madness. *Madness!* A child had literally fallen into her lap—what on earth was she supposed to do now?

What did one do with a child that simply appeared out of nowhere? Joy did not recall seeing a child with parents in the gardens as she had entered. In truth, she could not recall seeing anyone.

"What's your name?"

Joy ignored the girl's question, looking up at the snow-covered gardens around them. There was no one there.

This was impossible. Surely a child like this, evidently cared for, dressed in a warm coat and poorly tied hair ribbons, would have a parent, a governess, a guardian. Anyone!

Footsteps crunched on the snow, and Joy turned eagerly to look for the person to rescue her from this rather bizarre situation, but the man who turned the corner onto the path did not look as though he would have a child with him. The elderly gentleman shuffled past them with a cane, not giving Joy nor the child a second glance.

Before Joy could collect herself, consider what to say, the elderly gentleman was gone, leaving her alone with—

"I said, what's your name?"

Joy blinked down at the child, who had twisted in her lap and was now seated quite happily, looking up at her. What was she supposed to do now?

"Joy," she said stupidly.

Panic rose in her heart, twisting her lungs and churning her stomach. Was the girl a runaway? She did not look the sort to run from her home—but then, Joy reminded herself, what did that look like? Could one tell merely by looking?

"Joy," repeated the child. "That's a silly name."

"No it isn't," said Joy automatically.

Yes, she had heard it all, especially around this time of year. Tidings of comfort and joy, very witty—it was a bold gentleman indeed who suggested that Joy herself could be his comfort during these ice-cold days.

But she could not think about that, nor the upset she had left behind with her family…not while a stranger's child sat in her lap!

"My name is Paloma," said the girl, as though she introduced herself to strangers all the time. "It's a pretty name, don't you think?"

"Yes," said Joy hoarsely.

This was her own fault; somehow she had forced the universe, or God, or someone, to give her a child! What had she said?

I suppose I just need a family to fall into my lap this Christmas. Then I would fit in with the rest of the Fitzroys.

And just as she had been thinking about that, this girl *had*. And there were no ladies, no governesses about the place who could reasonably claim her. So where had she come from?

"Paloma," Joy said hesitantly. "Where…where did you come

from?"

The girl frowned, her face upside down as she looked up at Joy. "Come from?"

Joy swallowed. The girl could be no more than four or five, too young to understand, it seemed. But what was she going to do with her?

A smile danced across her features at the idea of taking the girl home. Why, she could just imagine the look on her parents' faces if she returned with a little girl. What would they say to her? What would they do to her?

"You're nice and warm," said the little girl, snuggling into Joy's arms. "I like you."

Joy's heart twisted, but it was with none of the fear nor panic that had ruled her mere moments ago. No, this was entirely new. Something deep, and powerful, and…maternal.

She would never have described herself in such a way, but then, she'd never had a child clamber into her lap so unaffectedly, so calmly, as though she belonged there.

"Paloma—"

"Paloma, there you are!"

Joy looked up. It was not a lady, nor a governess, who came panting around the corner, dragging a child who looked the absolute spitting image of the child in her lap.

No. It was a gentleman.

A gentleman, Joy realized, who was tall, with graying hair, all salt and pepper underneath his top hat, a poorly knitted scarf around his neck and a desperate look in his eye.

Ah.

"Paloma, what did I tell you about running off!" said the man as he stood by Joy's bench, breathing heavily—though not as heavily as the other child. "I thought I'd lost you!"

Before Joy could say anything, Paloma had slipped off her lap, giggling. "I found a new friend!"

"So you did," said the girl's father dryly.

Joy hurried to rise to her feet. A father of twins; goodness, he must be run off his feet. Did she not have the proof of the matter right before her?

"I-I am so sorry," she blurted out.

Where had that apology come from? But Joy felt it deep within her bones. One could not sit on benches with other people's children. Not without a formal introduction, anyway.

But the gentleman waved aside her apology with a dry laugh. "Please do not apologize. I am yet to teach my daughters any manners whatsoever, and I am afraid it is starting to show."

The other little girl giggled. "You're in trouble."

"No I'm not," retorted Paloma.

"That's enough of that from the pair of you," said their father swiftly, stepping between them. "Why don't you go and play there, where I can see you—*where I can see you*, Paloma—and I can apologize properly to this young lady."

The two girls scampered off, squealing with laughter as Paloma regaled her sister with her story, and Joy found herself standing awkwardly beside their father.

She swallowed. *Young lady.* She had ceased to be a young lady a good while ago; some of her fellow debutantes had children nearing eleven years old.

He was a charmer, then. Joy tried to look up at the gentleman without making it obvious she was looking at him, but this was near impossible. He was so close to her.

If only he wasn't so handsome.

The thought flashed through Joy's mind before she could take it captive, but there it was. If he wasn't so handsome, she could perhaps construct a sentence or two. Not witty ones; that would be too much to ask. But at least coherent ones.

What actually emerged from her mouth was: "Paloma."

"And Jemima, or Jemmy," he said with a wide grin as he looked over at his daughters. "Do not blame me. I had no choice on their names. My two turtle doves."

Joy's heart thundered most painfully in her chest. He was handsome; his eyes crinkled in the corners as he looked at his daughters, his jawline was accentuated when he smiled, and his hands were so close to hers…

Hands that showed a wedding ring.

Joy swallowed. Of course—she was an absolute fool to forget it. This man, whoever he was, was married. Paloma and Jemmy had a mother, inside in the warm at this time of year.

If only she had not noticed how handsome he was—or the ring, Joy thought wretchedly. Either way, she could have imagined the two of them having a…moment.

As it was…

"I have a cousin called Jemima," she said weakly.

Was that all she could manage?

"Indeed?" he said politely. "I am sorry that my little one got away from me. I will admit, having two this age has become more and more trying with every day."

Joy smiled awkwardly. "I can imagine."

Yes, you can imagine, said that horrible little voice in her head. *And you'll have to imagine, won't you? Because you'll never have a family like that.*

Her gaze drifted over to the girls playing some sort of tag game, and her stomach lurched. It was most unfair. Here she was, unmarried and without children, and some woman—this gentleman's wife—had two in one go.

"I hope she was not too much of a bother."

Joy turned back to the gentleman, and her stomach lurched for a very different reason. Goodness, he was almost intoxicatingly handsome. He was older than her, perhaps by a decade, but age had not withered his appearance, nor his charm.

A teasing smile danced across his face. "Apologies. I have not introduced myself."

"No," Joy said without thinking, "you have not."

The gentleman's smile broadened, and Joy flushed at having spoken so out of turn with a stranger. Her tongue would be the death of her one day! She never waited to speak, never thought about whether what she was about to say was appropriate.

But the gentleman did not seem to mind. Quite to the contrary: he was beaming.

Joy looked away, trying to focus on the slowly falling snow rather than the girls playing, or the gentleman who had quite quickly attracted her heart.

"Gilbert Kitteridge," he said with a bow. "At your service."

Joy curtseyed, hoping she did herself justice in the heavy pelisse and gloves, before realizing she had not given her own name. "Joy Fitzroy."

"Joy," said Gilbert with a wry smile. "I wished to call one of ours Joy."

A shiver rushed down Joy's spine. *Ours.*

Not ours, she told herself sternly. *Not actually ours, not Gilbert and mine. That's ridiculous. He's talking about his wife—his* wife, *Joy! Remember!*

The last thing she should do was forget that the handsome, charming man before her was wed.

"That's Joy!" said Paloma, grinning over at them. "She's got a silly name!"

"That's not very kind," called over Gilbert. "I must apologize for her. She is young."

Joy smiled weakly. How strange it was to hear such similar words from Gilbert—from Mr. Kitteridge's mouth as from her own parents'. There were just some girls, it appeared, not built to conform to the rules of Society.

"I do not mind," she said honestly. "I like to see a child who is direct and abrupt."

Gilbert chuckled, shaking his head and causing clumps of snow to fall from his hat. "I suppose I would rather have a daughter who could stick up for herself, ensure that no cad spoke to her inappropriately, than one who simply accepted what life threw at her."

Joy stared. "That...that is just how I think."

Their eyes met, but Joy quickly dropped her gaze to the snow-covered ground.

This was highly scandalous! True, they had met innocently enough, but she was speaking to a gentleman to whom she had not been formally introduced alone, unchaperoned—a married man!

Well, I'll just have to calm myself down, Joy told herself sternly. No thoughts of romance, no thoughts of their hands accidently touching, or the girls disappearing to leave them alone, of how Gilbert could take her in his arms and…

Blast. Joy swallowed, knowing she should leave, walk away while she could hold her head up high. She had not truly embarrassed herself yet. The clever thing to do would be to leave.

"And where is Mrs. Kitteridge?" Joy asked formally, attempting to force herself to focus on the fact that the rather delectable Mr. Kitteridge was entirely unavailable.

A shadow swept across Gilbert's face, and he hesitated before answering. "I am a widower, Mrs. Fitzroy."

Joy swallowed. *Oh, for the love of…*

She should have left. Now she was in not one, but two awkward situations, and she would have to attempt to untangle them both, for she could not now, in all conscience, leave before she did!

"I am so sorry," she said quietly, trying to meet his gaze but not quite managing it, instead looking at his lips. Kissable lips.

Get a hold of yourself, Joy Fitzroy!

"Thank you," Gilbert said softly. "I do not dwell on it."

Discomfort raged in Joy's heart. Of course he did not dwell on it! No man should have to discuss such a personal thing with a relative stranger—she should not have said a word.

Joy's gaze flicked over to the girls. Motherless children. No wonder Paloma had launched herself into her lap—they must be crying out for female companionship. What a shame she could not—

No. Joy took a deep breath and knew she had to clarify Gilbert's misconception.

And not, she told herself, because she had discovered he was a widower. Not at all. That had nothing to do with it. Almost nothing.

"*Miss* Fitzroy."

Gilbert frowned. "I beg your pardon?"

Joy sighed. "You thought I was married. I am not Mrs. Fitzroy—it's Miss Fitzroy."

Was that a spark of interest in his eyes—a fire that could be fanned to a flame?

But the moment Joy was certain she had seen something, it was gone. Whatever it was, it was a trick of the imagination. She certainly should not be hoping to see attraction in Gilbert—in Mr. Kitteridge's eyes. But what else could that be?

"Now it is my turn to apologize, again," said Gilbert with a dry laugh. "I merely assumed... Well. A woman such as your-self..."

Joy swallowed down the instinct to throw back an insult. Yes, a woman as old as her; it was natural that he believe her married already. Of course he did. Why wouldn't he?

"I mean, a woman as beautiful as you..."

Joy's jaw fell open as she looked up into Gilbert's face, then her cheeks flushed so hot, she was certain he would notice her absolute astonishment.

As beautiful as her? What was he talking about? Was it possible that...that Gilbert Kitteridge believed she was a married woman because she was...beautiful?

"I have offended you," Gilbert said hastily, his cheeks reddening. "I just meant—"

"I know what you meant," cut in Joy, heart pounding. "At least, I think I did. I..."

Why weren't words coming to her? She had never struggled to speak, always had something to say—something usually cutting, yes, but still. *Something.*

But in this moment, standing in the falling snow in Sydney Gardens with a handsome widower called Gilbert Kitteridge she had not even known twenty minutes ago...

Joy's mouth was dry, her heart still pounded, and there was something rather uncomfortable in her chest.

Gilbert cleared his throat. "I hope I have not offended you."

"Offended me?" Joy could not help but laugh dryly as she met his gaze. "I think that is the nicest thing anyone has ever said to me."

The moment held between them, a timeless moment, one full of rich emotion that Joy could not untangle.

But she did not need to. Understanding this moment, this look, this feeling welling up inside her did not need words, did not need to be dissected to be understood. It needed to be embraced, accepted, wallowed in.

A moment of pure happiness, of feeling right with the world, of knowing that she was precisely where she wanted to be. Precisely where she ought to be.

"Papa, look!"

And then the moment was over. Joy took a hesitant step back, not knowing how she had managed to move closer to Gilbert—to Mr. Kitteridge.

He turned to grin at his daughters. "Well done, I—Paloma Kitteridge, what have you done to your sister?"

Giggles echoed out around Sydney Gardens, and Joy could not help but laugh as she looked over herself.

There stood Paloma, a wide grin on her face, so like her father's...and Jemmy was lying on the ground, half buried in snow, giggling hard.

"Jemmy, are you—Come on, get up this instant." Gilbert strolled away to rescue one of his daughters from the other.

A half-understood surge of affection rushed through Joy. He was a good man—a good father. One who would be worth securing by any lady.

Joy shook her head as though that would dislodge the thought from her mind. No, she absolutely could not think that way; it was outrageous! She was not the sort of lady to go around hunting for a husband, and going after a widower? For all she knew, his wife died last week!

"Come on, we had better get you home," Gilbert said with a wry laugh. "Yes, I know she allowed you to do it, Paloma, but that does not mean... Miss Fitzroy?"

Joy looked up, startled. Why was it so wonderful to hear his name on her lips? "Yes?"

"We may have to venture home to warm up these rascals," said Gilbert with a laugh. "Do you have any plans this after—"

"Yes," said Joy automatically.

Why had she said that? Was Gilbert—Mr. Kitteridge about to invite her to his home for afternoon tea? Why had she so instantly prevented herself from going back with him?

Because, Joy told herself firmly, *that is not what ladies of the* ton *do*. They were not introduced! Not formally. By the rules of Society, she should not even be talking to him.

"I have to return home," she said, trying to smile. "Good day, Mr. Kitteridge, Miss Kitteridges."

The girls giggled as they clasped their hands around their father's legs, and Joy tried her absolute best to leave Sydney Gardens without looking back at the family that had so intrigued her.

And she managed it. Just about. At least, she only looked back three times.

Each time, the girls were racing around their father, returning to their game of tag, utterly focused on catching each other.

Their father simply stood and stared after her. Joy tried not to smile.

He thought she was beautiful.

CHAPTER THREE

"Ah, she's here!"

Joy managed to put a smile on her face as a lady entered the drawing room.

Harmony, on the other hand, was far more effusive. "Isabella!"

Rising from her seat by the fire, Harmony strode toward their cousin, and Joy attempted to keep the smile on her face from faltering.

"It really is too kind of you to invite me to visit," Isabella Fitzroy said with a smile as her aunt and cousin fussed over her. "Oh, thank you."

Joy watched as her cousin was warmly welcomed by the Bath contingent of the Fitzroy family: her father standing up to give her his armchair, her mother clucking over Isabella, taking her coat, Harmony asking a thousand and one questions Isabella simply could not respond to.

"And how are the Chalcroft Fitzroys? How is Aunt Leonora? I suppose she is busy making the last of the presents for the servants—and Kitty, she is definitely coming to Chalcroft for Christmas?"

Laughter and chatter filled the drawing room, and Joy knew she should rise to her feet, welcome her cousin for the short visit she was making to them.

Goodness, she could hardly remember the last time Isabella had been here. A recluse was not quite the right word for her, but it was not far off. Isabella, the only other unmarried Fitzroy, was not one to frequent Bath nor London, preferring to stay at Chalcroft.

And what's not to like? Joy thought darkly. A wild manor house in the countryside, the farm just next door and plenty of woodlands to walk in with no fear of being caught unchaperoned with a gentleman…

Blast.

"I mean, a woman as beautiful as you…"

Joy's smile flickered, though she attempted to keep up with the conversation.

"—so elegant. Is that the new style in Bath?"

"Oh, this?" Harmony laughed. "No, this is just what my lady's maid can do with my hair in the five minutes before Rufus needs me! He is most charming; he—Here he is!"

Rufus scampered in, a gingerbread man in each hand and crumbs all round his mouth.

"There's my grandson!" Rupert left his niece and rushed toward Rufus, arms wide.

The child giggled raucously and rushed around the armchair, and the room laughed.

Joy remembered to laugh just in time. Harmony's eyes had fallen on her, she could feel them, and she knew it was very poor manners not to laugh at the antics of her nephew. He was, after all, but eighteen months old and a true delight.

At least, that was what everyone kept telling her.

"Joy, will you not welcome our guest?" asked her mother pointedly.

"Yes, of course," said Joy hastily, rising to her feet. "Wonderful to see you, Isabella."

The dark-haired woman kissed Joy's cheek. "Do not worry. I shall not keep you long."

Her whisper was just about audible to Joy, and made very

little sense. *Not keep me long?*

"Now, sit down, Isabella, and we will get you some tea," said Frances distractedly as Harmony rushed off to attempt to catch her son. "Tea, tea… Ring the bell, will you, Joy?"

Joy tried not to roll her eyes as she stepped over her nephew and around her father, avoiding tripping over Harmony as she pulled the bell by the fireplace. Really, it was a zoo in here! And she was the one often criticized for being a poor host!

"I hope you do not mind the chaos. It comes with having children about the place," said Joy's mother with a laugh—a laugh that swiftly died as she looked up into the eyes of Joy and Isabella.

Joy rolled her eyes. Well, really. It was not as though either she or her cousin had asked for the topic of marriage and children to be avoided, even if it did sting—but to make such a fuss about it when the subject had been broached…

It drew far more attention to the thing than she would have wanted, and from the fixed smile on Isabella's face, her cousin felt the same way.

"Oh, do not worry about it, please," Isabella said softly, sitting down in an armchair. "You should see Chalcroft most of the time—absolutely *littered* with children!"

Joy sat opposite her cousin, keeping her gaze low. She could hear the tension in Isabella's voice, even if she did not wish it to be obvious. There was pain there. Well, it had been about two years since those horrible rumors were printed about Isabella, hadn't it? Cruel they had been, and some in the family whispered it was Maria's own husband who—But no, that couldn't be right.

"Yes, how are your sisters?" asked Frances, recovering from her faux pas and seating herself as her husband and daughter rushed about after Rufus, who knocked over a small console table in the corner. "They are well?"

The conversation managed to continue without any further upset, and Joy was able to retreat once more into her thoughts. Her memories.

"I mean, a woman as beautiful as you…"

She shivered, as though she was once again standing in the cold snow with Gilbert Kitteridge and his daughters. He had called her beautiful.

Which was nonsense, of course. *He was merely being polite*, Joy told herself firmly. There was no other reason why a man like him could have said such a thing. He was attempting to make up for his awkward assumption that she was married; that was all.

Gilbert Kitteridge. She had never been introduced to him before…but for some reason, Joy felt as though the name was familiar. If only she knew more about him. How old he was, where he came from, how long he had lived in Bath—if he even lived here. Perhaps he was here for the Season.

Was he a gentleman? From the little Joy could remember, he had been dressed as an elegant, handsome man. He surely could not be in trade.

And when had his wife died? Had he loved her?

Joy tried to push those particular thoughts aside. It was not right, thinking such things about a gentleman. He had undoubtedly loved his wife, keenly mourned her. Now she came to think about it, his greatcoat had been black. Perhaps he was still in mourning.

The point was, Joy thought darkly, he was certainly not interested in her. Not like that.

"Don't you think?"

Joy blinked. Isabella was looking at her as though expecting an answer, as Harmony hoisted Rufus in her arms. The boy was upside down, giggling boisterously.

"I-I beg your pardon?"

"I said I think it is a marvelous day—the weather, I mean," said Isabella with a swift smile that just as swiftly disappeared. "I think I may go for a walk in town."

"Ah, what a shame we cannot accompany you!" said Joy's mother. "Your uncle and I have a prior engagement."

But Isabella raised her hand. "Please, do not apologize. After the noise and rush of Chalcroft, it would be pleasant to be…well, on my own, for an hour or two. I intend to return to Chalcroft this afternoon."

Joy glanced surreptitiously at her mother. That had not been her mother's plan at all—Isabella had been expected to stay at least a week, then return with them to Chalcroft for the family Christmas celebrations. At least, if Frances had her way.

But she was nothing if not gracious. "Of course. You know the way?"

Isabella nodded as she rose. "I do indeed."

Joy inclined her head to her cousin. They were not very alike, really, but circumstances had pushed them together, and there was a strange sort of affection and respect between them.

Isabella laughed. "You know, it is so strange. I truly did not believe you would permit me to walk on my own!"

Joy's father shrugged as he pulled Rufus from Harmony's arms and carried him, still upside down, to an armchair, where he deposited the boy in a giggling lump. "You are old enough to know what is appropriate, Isabella, and you have been to Bath countless times. Do you believe you need a chaperone?"

"No," said Isabella with a wry smile.

Joy thought her markedly controlled; she was not sure what she would say if one of her uncles had pointed out her age in public.

"My father was terrified of me coming into town, but I must say, I feel a great deal more relaxed," admitted Isabella as she stepped to the door. "It was pleasant to see you all."

The door closed behind her.

"Now what did—" began Joy.

Her mother held up a hand, and Joy halted. Only after a few moments, when the front door had opened and closed, did Frances lower her hand.

"Well!" she said with wide eyes. "Was that to be our visit with Isabella?"

"I believe so, Mama," said Joy. She had to admit, she was

impressed. Isabella had demonstrated it was quite possible to be given directions by a Fitzroy parent, then entirely ignore them. How fascinating.

"I hoped she would be staying with us near a week," said Rupert mildly. "Not stopping in for less than an hour."

His wife nodded. "So did I! But Isabella has a different idea. Interesting."

Joy glanced out the window, wondering what Isabella could be up to. The thought itself was ridiculous; Fitzroys did not *get up to* things.

"Well, I had better leave too," said Harmony with a sigh. "I promised the neighbors I would take Rufus over this morning, give their two someone else to play with."

Joy rolled her eyes as their parents looked affectionately at Harmony. As if she was the only one who did anything pleasant, or kind! Just because Joy did not parade it around...

"That's thoughtful of you, dear," said Frances with a warm smile. "How are they?"

"Oh, as well as can be expected," Harmony said, sighing heavily. "Come on, then, you scamp! Time to put your coat on."

Joy breathed out a slow sigh of relief as Rufus and Harmony started toward the hall. A bit of peace and quiet, that was what she needed. The whole household had been in uproar at the expected arrival of Isabella, and now that she was not staying even a day—even a full hour—it would be nice for things to return to normal. At least for a week. Until they left for Chalcroft.

"Come on, Joy."

Joy looked up. "I beg your pardon?"

Harmony was tying the ribbon of her bonnet from the door-way. "I thought you could come with me."

Go with her? She must be out of her wits, thought Joy. A morning of watching children play—only one of which she actually knew? Had Harmony ever *met* her?

"Why do you need me there?" Joy said stiffly, clasping the arms of her chair as though she was about to be dragged off. "It's all parents together, isn't it?"

Harmony frowned. "Christmas is a time for family, Joy Fitzroy, and I've seen precious little of you so far, and at Chalcroft I'll have even less chance to talk to you. Come on."

And with that, she turned back to the hall, as though the conversation was over.

Which it certainly wasn't. "I have no desire to watch someone's poxy children—"

"Joy Fitzroy!" exclaimed her mother. "*Rufus!*"

Joy sighed. It was so much easier when her nephew was so small that he could not talk. One could say whatever one wished, then.

"I have no wish to go," Joy said quietly.

"Nonsense," said her father with a smile. "Off you go."

"You only want me to go so you'll get the best seat to read in by the fire."

"Joy!"

"Fine!" Joy rose to her feet, seething, but unable to do anything about it.

If her parents wanted her to go, fine, she would go. If Harmony wanted her to accompany her, fine, she would. But she did not have to enjoy it.

Only a smidgen of embarrassment seared Joy's heart as she pulled on her pelisse and gloves. She knew why they were doing it, of course. Her parents and her sister.

They felt sorry for her.

And that was the worst part of the whole story. It wasn't enough that they thought she stayed at home too much, spoke too much in company, was too sarcastic. It was that they felt sorry for her. Poor, unmarried Joy.

"Come on, then," she said heavily as she stomped out of the house, Harmony and Rufus behind her. "Let's go."

The snow had melted to dangerous ice overnight, and Joy found herself slipping and sliding as the three of them made their way across town to where Harmony and David lived. A pretty little house, one that Joy would rather like for herself—not that she had ever admitted it.

But instead of walking up the short path Joy knew so well, Harmony led the way up the path to the house next door. Just as pretty, just as elegant, but with a green door instead of a red one.

Harmony lifted the knocker and rapped out a complex rhythm.

"Do you have to do that?" Joy found herself muttering.

Her sister's cheeks tinged. "What?"

"Make everything so musical," teased Joy under her breath, hoping Rufus did not hear.

The door opened and a maid took their pelisses, bonnets, and gloves from them.

"I do not make everything musical," said Harmony under her breath as she smoothed down her skirts then reached out for Rufus' hand.

Joy grinned as they stepped toward a door that could only be to the drawing room. "Yes you do. You know you do!"

Harmony's cheeks flushed a darker red. "No I—Ah, Mr. Kitteridge."

Joy blinked. *No.* It was not possible.

It could not be Gilbert Kitteridge standing before her; it was a mirage. A mistake. A dream that had moved from her night into her day. He could not be standing before her.

"Joy," he blurted out, staring with wide eyes.

Joy swallowed. She was not going to make a fool of herself—and she certainly wasn't going to give Harmony any reason to run back to their parents with tales. *Probably.*

"Good morning, Mr. Kitteridge," she said formally, curtseying.

She was not going to look at Harmony, who, she was certain, was staring at both of them in absolute confusion.

How was this possible? Gilbert Kitteridge and his daughters…Harmony's neighbors?

Perhaps that was why the name was so familiar. Well, it was

not as though Harmony gossiped—it was not in her nature—but at one time or another, she must have mentioned the Kitteridges. That was why Joy knew the name. Oh, this was a disaster!

"Joy!"

Joy swallowed. Paloma and Jemmy were lying on the rug by the fireplace, playing with dolls they had cut out of paper.

"Hello," she said weakly.

"Joy?" repeated Harmony, staring wide-eyed at her sister.

"Joy—Miss Fitzroy," amended Gilbert hastily.

Joy waited for the floor to swallow her up, but disobligingly, it did no such thing. Oh, this was so embarrassing! Now she would have to answer awkward questions, face her sister's teasing about knowing such a handsome gentleman, and worst of all...

A shiver of panic rushed down her spine. *Her mother's questions.*

"Rufus, careful!"

Harmony's attention was immediately taken by her son, who rushed toward the twins with a giggle...leaving Joy standing by the door with Gilbert beside her.

"I did not know... I mean..." Joy swallowed. Why was it so difficult to speak? Why did the man's mere presence make her all hot and tingly? "I did not know you were acquainted with Harmony."

"I did not know you knew her either," replied Gilbert quietly.

Joy smiled feebly. "She is my sister."

"Ah. I have always known her as Mrs. Navarre," he pointed out as the noise by the fireplace increased. "I did not know she was your sister."

"Yes," said Joy, with a teasing smile on her face from she knew not where. "But I am the pretty one."

"Yes. Yes, I can see that."

She stared, hardly able to believe he had said such a thing— and it appeared he was just as surprised. A dark tinge covered his cheeks, and Gilbert clutched his hands together, looking down at them.

Was he teasing her? Was, perhaps, his comment only yesterday about her being beautiful only a jest as well? Had she, in fact, managed to tie herself in knots over a mere jest?

"So you are Rufus' aunt."

Joy could not help it; she looked at Gilbert and tried to work out just how much she would have to move for her fingertips to brush up against his own. "I am."

"I have heard a great many stories about you," said Gilbert.

Joy groaned. "Goodness, please, don't believe half of them."

What on earth could Rufus—or Harmony—have told him?

"Even if I only believed a quarter of them, I would wish to know you."

Had she heard that correctly? From what Joy could see, there was no teasing in his expression; Gilbert Kitteridge was being earnest.

She swallowed. This was getting out of hand. She was very close to flirting—flirting!—with a widowed gentleman. A gentleman she barely knew. A gentleman who was Harmony's neighbor! That, surely, was enough reason to attempt to calm down.

"Your daughters," said Joy. "They are well?"

Gilbert smiled wearily. "Well practiced in the art of exhausting me, I must say. But then, I would not trade my two turtle doves for anything."

Joy's heart twisted. *Two turtle doves*—such an adorable way for a father to speak about his daughters. As one of two sisters herself, she knew the importance of having a father who would stand by you, support you, love you unconditionally. It was pleasant to see Gilbert was such a man.

It was more than pleasant. It caused a searing heat to blossom across her chest, making every inch tingle. It was not unwelcome, just unexpected, uncontrolled.

Joy did not understand it.

"They are lucky to have you," she said, flushing at the intimate way she spoke.

Gilbert smiled. "I think I am lucky to have them—and lucky that they have brought you into my life. As it were."

And then it happened. Joy was not entirely sure how it had happened—she was not conscious of having moved an inch—but somehow Gilbert's hand brushed up against hers.

And there it was, fiery flames, heat and desire and lust and everything she had never felt, unlocked in a moment, pouring from his hand to her heart, and Joy's lips parted at the suddenness of it all.

She wanted him. Wanted him to touch her again, wanted to know what it was like to caress that salt-and-pepper hair, kiss those lips…to know what it was to be desired by a gentleman.

"Joy?" Gilbert breathed.

Joy swallowed. The feelings did not die away, not exactly, but they dimmed enough for her to realize just what was happening. She was standing in a room with Gilbert…and his two daughters. And Harmony. And Rufus.

This should not be happening—at least, Joy thought wildly, a little mischievousness soaring into her soul, it should not be happening *here*.

No, she needed Gilbert on his own, in a poorly lit room, where they knew they would not be disturbed…

"Gilbert," she breathed.

"Gilbert, could you give me a hand here?" came Harmony's voice.

Joy watched Gilbert's jaw tighten. Oh, if only her sister had not spoken. If only she could have permitted them just a few more minutes!

Then he smiled wearily. "Never the right moment," he whispered, then, in a stronger voice, "Coming, Mrs. Navarre."

Joy carefully reached out for the wall beside her as Gilbert walked away from her toward the chattering by the fireplace. What had just happened? And most importantly…how could she make sure it happened again?

CHAPTER FOUR

J OY SIGHED HEAVILY as the carriage pulled up outside the house. She had not intended to be running late—but then, did anyone?

"Sorry, Harmony," she muttered as the wintry air seeped into the carriage while she waited outside her sister's home. "Sorry…"

Harmony always hated it when she was late. It was a habit Joy was not particularly proud of, but she still could not understand how some people were always…on time. On time? Did they not have anything else to do in their lives, that they just appeared when expected?

Truth be told, Joy knew she should not have started that book only half an hour before she was due to pick Harmony up in the Fitzroy carriage. The sweeping pages had entirely captivated her, making it impossible to hear the chiming of the clock.

Joy smiled wryly in the silence of the carriage. *Well. Not entirely.* She had heard the clock, but immediately discounted it as something not worth attending to.

And now they were late. Late to a concert! Harmony's absolute worst nightmare. Joy knew she would be faced with a great many complaints when her sister finally deigned to leave her house and step into the carriage.

Another sigh escaped her lips. She would just have to endure it.

After a few minutes, however, Joy peered out of the carriage window up at Harmony's home. There was no sign of her. It was most unlike Harmony to be running late herself, and this was a concert for which she had specifically requested Joy's presence.

"You will absolutely love it," she had said as Joy groaned, rolling her eyes. "No, truly, Joy! I believe you will understand the true passion of the cello thanks to the…"

She had continued speaking, but Joy could not entirely recall what she said.

But here she was, only…maybe fifteen minutes late? Joy had expected to find Harmony standing on the pavement, tutting, tapping her feet in that irritating rhythm she always had.

But her sister was nowhere to be seen.

The Fitzroy driver poked his head in the door. "Shall I knock, miss?"

Joy nodded. "Thank you, Andrews."

It was most unaccountable. Unless she was ill? Harmony always had an iron constitution, but Joy supposed there was a first time for everything.

Footsteps. Andrews had returned. "Just a minute, miss."

Joy sighed deeply, nodded, and tutted as the driver clambered back onto the carriage.

The next time Joy was late—and for a perfectly good reason; she always had a reason—she would remind Harmony of this moment if her sister dared to complain. They were late to the concert, and Harmony hated walking into a concert while the music was playing.

Joy could not understand—

But there were footsteps. Joy shifted to the side of the carriage, ensuring her gown was pulled over, and grinned. If sisters could not tease sisters, what was the world coming to?

"Well, about time!" Joy said in a mock-haughty voice, tutting just as their mother did when she was truly aggravated. "I have been waiting these last ten…ten…"

It was not often words failed Joy, but it had been happening with peculiar regularity recently, and it happened again. At least this time she knew why.

Instead of Harmony's delicate hand and quiet apologies, a large, strong hand opened the carriage door and Gilbert Kitteridge stepped inside.

Joy stared, all the breath knocked out of her.

This cannot be—this is not possible. She had believed herself calm under pressure, but evidently she had never experienced a surprise like this one.

Gilbert settled himself in the carriage opposite her, for which Joy was very thankful. The idea of such a gentleman seated beside her, in an otherwise empty carriage…

No, it was too much. Her body was tingling at the thought of such an indiscretion. Who knew what might happen if he had actually—But he had not, Joy reminded herself forcefully, and nothing untoward was going to happen.

She did not *think* it would.

Why he was here, however, was yet to be determined.

"Y-you," she spluttered.

Her cheeks warmed at her inarticulate noises. She was a witty, elegant, charming woman! At least, Joy attempted to tell herself that as her splutters descended into silence and she fixed her eyes on the man before her.

This was…impossible. There could not be a gentleman here, let alone Gilbert Kitteridge, a man she had attempted not to think about since his sudden role as Harmony's neighbor only yesterday.

But the trouble was, she could not pretend Gilbert was Harmony. Harmony was gentle, kind, soft-hearted, petite…and most definitely her sister.

But Gilbert: Gilbert was all man. It was only now that she was in a carriage with him that Joy realized just how tall he was, how broad, how masculine in his looks and scent. The carriage suddenly felt small, her own half shrinking and shrinking until Joy felt as though she was seated right beside him.

Which she wasn't, of course. That would be outrageous.

Still. Their knees were only a few inches away.

"Me," said Gilbert with a wry smile. "I must apologize for not being your sister. I am sure she would have been a far more pleasant companion."

Joy simply stared. Pleasant wasn't the problem; pleasure at his presence was—not that she was about to announce it to him.

The question was, why on earth had her sister's neighbor, instead of her sister, entered the carriage? And how would she manage to retrieve her tongue to ask him such a question?

Thankfully, Gilbert seemed to realize there was a need for explanation. "Mrs. Navarre wasn't feeling well—a headache."

"A headache," repeated Joy blankly.

Headache? Harmony did not have headaches—at least, not since…

Joy's stomach twisted painfully. Not since she was carrying Rufus. Was it possible, after so many years of waiting for a child, that Harmony and David had fallen for a second?

But she could not think of that now, and she certainly would not ask Harmony when she next saw her. Joy had learned enough about the indiscretion of asking a woman about her childbearing when her sister first struggled to conceive.

No, she had to concentrate on the first problem before her: Gilbert Kitteridge.

"Thank you," Joy said, a little stiffly. Well, she could not let him see just how he affected her, could she? "For giving me my sister's message."

"I am afraid I bring more news than that," he continued with a grin. "Your sister regaled me with such detail about this concert—the cellos, apparently, are going to change my life—that she agreed to watch my turtle doves while I took her place by your side."

By your side.

Joy swallowed. He did not mean it like that. He probably did not even hear the way it sounded, that intimate, delightful way it tripped off his tongue so naturally.

She tried to ignore the lurch her stomach gave, tried not to look at his lips. She was not going to form a foolish attachment to Gilbert Kitteridge, Joy told herself firmly.

"I beg your pardon?"

Joy looked up. Goodness, had she said any of that aloud? "I said, oh."

Gilbert waited, then nodded awkwardly. "Yes. Right. Good. Shall…shall we go?"

Joy looked at him helplessly. She could hardly say no, could she? There was no possibility of such rudeness; she could not demand he leave the carriage and go to the concert alone.

Besides, even if it was within the bounds of decorum…she did not wish to. An afternoon with Gilbert Kitteridge, at a concert. In public, with no hint of scandal, Joy reminded herself. A perfectly suitable companion.

And he was a widow.

"I think it ridiculous, that is all. The only people who are able to do what they like are widows and widowers. They can bed whom they like…"

Joy shivered at the memory of her own words not two days ago. Yes, widows and widowers were perfectly suited to scandal; no one would suspect them, and they had far more opportunity to do whatever they wished.

Whatever they wished…

"Miss Fitzroy?"

Joy jerked to attention. Her mind had wandered into avenues it certainly should not be. Young ladies—*all* ladies—should not be thinking of a naked gentleman when they were sitting right before him in a carriage. Fully clothed. *Unfortunately.*

"Yes," she said a little uncertainly, and then, with more feeling, "Yes. Drive on."

She tapped the roof as she spoke. The carriage pulled away, jerking slightly, and Joy put out a hand to prevent herself sliding across. It would not matter usually, of course, but with Gilbert there, such a movement would have brushed her knees against his.

An innocuous touch, perhaps, but Joy was not sure whether any touch by Gilbert—Mr. Kitteridge—could be described as innocuous. Or innocent.

Indeed, her entire body seemed to be quivering just at his presence.

Joy swallowed. She needed to say something, anything! Conversation was imperative; it had to be better than this awkward silence.

But no topic that could not be taken as something indecent appeared in her mind, which was undoubtedly a representation of her state of mind, rather than what could actually happen. Wild thoughts of kissing passionately in the carriage, of not going to the concert at all, just sitting here, kissing…

"Miss Fitzroy?"

Joy looked up. Her gaze had drifted to her hands as she indulged in daydreams she certainly could never repeat, and she was surprised to see a smile on Gilbert's face.

Her cheeks flushed. As though he knew what she had been thinking.

"Yes?" Joy said.

Gilbert's eyebrows rose just a fraction. "It's just…we are here."

Joy glanced out of the carriage and saw to her surprise that he was quite right. They were here. The Assembly Rooms were far closer to Harmony's home than her own, of course, but Joy had barely noticed time passing.

"Miss Fitzroy?"

"Yes, yes, right," said Joy hurriedly, allowing herself to be helped out of the carriage by Andrews, thankful—and disappointed—that it had not been Gilbert's hand. "Right. Good. We are here."

"We are indeed."

Gilbert's voice was just behind Joy's, so close she almost started. He must be but an inch behind her! Trying not to think about what she would feel if she took a gentle step back, or even leaned back, Joy stepped forward.

"I think we have not missed too much," she said lightly to the air in general.

They had not. At least, as far as Joy could tell. Harmony would have been able to describe, in painstaking detail, just what they had missed from the first twenty minutes of the concert and decry the shame of it for far too long.

As it was, Joy could barely concentrate on the music as they sat. It was there, she was aware of it, filling the air and indeed demonstrating just what a cello could do.

But her senses were entirely taken over by the gentleman beside her.

Gilbert Kitteridge. Just by sitting beside her, doing nothing but breathing and listening to the concert, he was completely taking over Joy's ability to think, to breathe, to be.

His hands were by his sides, and Joy was uncomfortably aware of how close the chairs were—that his arm and her arm were touching. Why, if she just moved her hands a few inches, her right would touch his left.

Which she would not do. That was an outlandish thing to do on purpose—the sort of thing a harlot would do. A wanton woman. *Joy Fitzroy,* she told herself sternly, *you are not a wanton woman.*

Or a wanted woman, that cruel voice inside her whispered. *No one wants you, Joy. Gilbert certainly does not.*

And then his hand was moving, and for a terrible instant Joy's heart lurched and she was certain, absolutely certain, he was reaching for her hand, and she had already started to think how she would explain such an indiscretion to her parents—

Gilbert brought his hands together. He was clapping. Everyone was clapping.

Joy blinked. Applause was echoing around the Assembly Rooms as the musicians rose to bow to their audience.

It was over. The concert was over. Had her mind been so

overwhelmed with Gilbert's presence that she had not taken in a single moment?

"Miss Fitzroy?"

Joy swallowed. Gilbert was looking at her with…a smile. She could not recall the last gentleman who had done such a thing. Had *any* gentleman ever done such a thing?

It was not as though she was ostracized from Society—quite the opposite. Joy knew she was a welcome guest in most of the best homes in Bath, a constant presence on invitation lists, and had not yet been scolded in public by Lady Romeril, which was an achievement.

But no gentleman had come knocking for her, wishing to speak to her parents.

Joy had grown accustomed to it over time. At least, she thought she had.

Now she was looking into Gilbert's eyes and seeing something that could be mistaken for desire. For something dark, and deep, and dangerous.

"Miss Fitzroy?" he repeated.

"Yes?" she breathed.

"Are you ready to leave?"

"Leave?"

The noise of chairs moving, gowns swishing, footsteps around them suddenly rushed into her ears, and Joy saw with embarrassment that they were among the last to remain in their seats. The concert was over. Time to return home or to other engagements later in the evening.

Joy rose so swiftly she almost unbalanced herself. "Yes. Yes, time to leave."

She said nothing as she and Gilbert stepped through the elegant corridors. What could she say? Her entire mind was flooded with images, hopes, dreams unsuitable to speak aloud, and for some reason, that was all she could think of.

The cool air revived her. Joy took a deep breath in as she looked up at the sky. It was snowing again, only lightly as the sun dipped below the hills and long shadows streaked the pavement.

"Miss Fitzroy, it is such a lovely evening," said Gilbert. "I thought…maybe… Well. Would you like to walk back?"

Joy looked into his dark eyes, full of an emotion she did not recognize.

She wanted to say yes, but knew that was impossible. Walk home with a gentleman to whom she was not engaged? She still had not formally been introduced, though she supposed now she had been inside his house, there was little point in doing so.

Her stomach lurched painfully as her heart skipped a beat. She should say no. She should not walk alone with Gilbert Kitteridge.

"Yes, thank you," Joy heard herself say. "That would be pleasant."

Pleasant? Pleasant! Oh, if only she had got her words in order, but it was too late.

Despite her idiocy, there was a smile creeping across Gilbert's face. "Wonderful."

Without asking, without saying another word, he took her hand in his, placed it on his arm, and started to walk.

Joy's mouth was dry, and thankfully it did not appear that Gilbert expected her to speak. This was…wonderful. The warmth of his arm, the strength. The closeness now she was so inter-twined with him… Oh, that this walk could last forever.

"So," said Gilbert eventually as they reached the end of the street and turned a corner. "What did you think of the music?"

Joy laughed, releasing the tension building in her chest. "Oh, do not ask me. Harmony is the musical one in our family. She will be the one to tell you all about the impressive cellos."

"I am sure she could and will," Gilbert said with a laugh, "but I asked your opinion."

Heat spread across Joy's cheeks, and she hoped the fading light hid their color. She could not recall the last time a gentle-man had asked her opinion about such a thing. Except her father, of course, who certainly did not count.

"I do not think anyone has asked my opinion about music before," she admitted.

Gilbert raised an eyebrow. "Truly?"

"In fact," Joy said, feeling a little twisting discomfort in her chest but forcing herself on, "I do not think anyone has asked anything about me in ages. Not since Rufus was born."

"I do not know why. You are beautiful."

Embarrassment seared Joy's chest, and she dropped her gaze to the pavement before them as she attempted to collect herself.

"You are beautiful."

How was he able to say that, so calmly, so off the cuff? Joy did not understand how a gentleman who had met her but days ago felt bold enough to say such a thing! And yet he said it not in a teasing way. Just…calmly. As though it was a fact, irrefutable and inarguable.

Joy swallowed. "I suppose I am nothing compared to your wife."

Her heart entirely stopped.

What had possessed her to say such a thing? It was unconscionable; it was madness; it was ridiculous and foolish and shameful!

Her stomach sinking, Joy attempted to pull her arm away, but Gilbert held it fast.

"I think you are…very different," he said softly.

Joy glanced at his face. There was no hurt there, no grief—at least as she would expect to see it. His calm response gave her boldness she knew she should certainly not have, and before she knew it, a question had slipped from her lips.

"What happened to her?"

Gilbert sighed, his breath blossoming into the cold air as they turned off onto a smaller street, one with far fewer people.

"She died giving birth to my turtle doves. Twins, you know. Very dangerous—they told us that when the doctor suspected it was not one but two babes."

Joy waited to see if there was any more, but it did not appear there was—and in a way, she was relieved. Not merely because she was not certain whether she could hold her tongue, but because they were now on his street. She could make out Harmony's home from here, which meant they were but minutes away from his own.

The pavements were silent, with no one else in the freezing cold air as the sun threatened to entirely disappear. The stars were starting to come out now, dazzling in sudden brightness.

"I am so sorry," murmured Joy.

"Thank you," said Gilbert quietly as they stopped by his gate. "It was years ago now, of course. I never thought, in that moment, I would ever meet anyone I would wish to marry again."

Joy swallowed. That she could believe. "Well, I—"

She could say no more—not because her words had failed her again, but because Gilbert Kitteridge's lips were on hers.

The kiss was sudden, intoxicating, warm, far more than Joy had ever imagined a kiss could be. He had not grabbed her, had not pulled her into his arms—this was a mere instinct, a rush of movement and then his lips on hers.

Joy's eyelashes fluttered shut as she attempted to take in the overwhelming sensations of a gentleman's lips on hers—of Gilbert's kiss.

It was warm, yet desperate. She could taste an ache in him, a desire she had never known and could not match. Not yet. Not before knowing so much more. But as his tongue teased her lips, Joy found herself parting them, letting him in.

A small moan grew in her throat. This was everything: her whole body was alight, on fire for him, and she was discovering parts of her she had never known before—

And then it was over.

Joy gasped, trying to take in enough air after such an encounter. Gilbert was giving her a strange look.

"What…what was that for?" Joy managed to ask, heart pounding.

"I never thought, in that moment, I would ever meet anyone I would wish to marry again."

Gilbert shrugged. "I found someone."

CHAPTER FIVE

F OR THE FIRST time in a very long time, an excited sort of twist was occurring in Joy's stomach with every step she took along Terrace Walk.

Bath was busy. Perhaps because it was almost Christmas, and half of England was visiting the town; perhaps because snow was once again swirling, coating doors, windows, roofs, tree branches with its delicate white powder; perhaps because everyone appeared to be in such a hurry.

A smile crept across Joy's face, unbidden and wide. There was excitement in the air, merry calls to friends and acquaintances, carolers standing on a corner singing "The First Noel," the smell of roasted chestnuts in the air…

In short, everything designed to make one feel happy.

But that was not why Joy was contented. The memory of yesterday had not stopped repeating in her mind, and each time she revisited the moment, it seemed to grow in importance, in weight…in meaning.

"I never thought, in that moment, I would ever meet anyone I would wish to marry again."

"I found someone."

Joy brought her gloved hands together before her as she walked smartly down the pavement, dodging a pair of children playing some sort of hopping game.

Gilbert Kitteridge. A gentleman she had not known a week ago—even less!—and who was now entirely taking over her thoughts.

Not that she should let him. Joy was more than aware that ladies should not hope for such things from gentlemen—anything. Marriage, kisses, favors…it was not right.

That did not stop her, however.

"I found someone."

"Careful, miss!"

Joy was forced to take a hurried step off the pavement—right into the path of a barouche—thanks to the rude way a man strode forcefully out of a shop.

"Whoa there! Watch where you're going, miss!" the driver of the barouche called out.

Joy merely smiled. Nothing could dampen her spirits, not today, and if she was not very much mistaken, her destination would only bring her greater delight and happiness.

"Be careful yourself," she shot back to both men who had affronted her, and continued on her merry way.

She was attending the Pump Room.

It had been quite a few weeks since Joy had deigned to attend the Pump Room. *A spectator sport for those who had nothing better to do*, she described it to her parents, and they had sighed at her cynicism.

And she had been right. Joy was tired of being trotted out to such a place, signing her name in the visitors book, then parading around and around, as though she had nothing better to do, gazing at people who had no interest in her and receiving their gazes in return.

Perhaps if she had an interest in fashion, she would have enjoyed the opportunities to gaze at what the ladies of the *ton* were wearing, compare them to London fashions—details of which were provided by the London Fitzroy cousins—and deride those gowns she did not like.

But that was not Joy's style. No, she would rather be having a pleasant conversation, and that simply could not be found in the Pump Room.

But today…

"Well, yes, Mr. Kitteridge is often at the Pump Room for an hour or so in the morning," Harmony had told her sister with surprise that morning. "Why do you ask?"

Joy had been forced to lie in that moment, which she had not particularly liked, but there was no possibility of her revealing the truth.

Because he kissed me, she would certainly not say.

Because he looked at me as though I was special. Important.

Because when he touches me, I feel…

Everything, thought Joy ruefully as she entered the Pump Room, feeling the warmer temperature with so many people packed in the place. *As though the entire world centers on us.*

It was a heady sensation, and one she was eager to repeat. And so, to the Pump Room.

The place was indeed so crowded that, for a moment, Joy was not certain whether she would be able to distinguish him even if he was here. Gentlemen's top hats glided around the room like ships, with a few feathers and far more bonnets accompanying them.

Everyone seemed to have arrived in pairs.

A twist of discomfort troubled Joy's stomach. Well, she was no stranger to wandering around Bath alone—there was never any trouble from footpads or the like, not really. But here, in such a social sphere, it was a little odd to be on her own.

She caught the gaze of an impertinent young man looking at her most unabashedly. Joy turned her head slightly in case he was staring at someone behind her, but there was no one there but an elderly gentleman snoozing in a chair.

Joy turned back to the stranger, who winked at her.

Feeling heat flushing her cheeks and hoping to goodness that if Gilbert was here he had not seen such a thing, Joy stepped as determinedly as she could to the visitors book.

It was open. Myriad names swam in front of Joy's eyes as she attempted to concentrate while her heart started to beat frantically.

This was it. She was about to see whether he was here.

A name caught her eye, but not for the reason she had intended.

Miss Isabella Fitzroy

Joy stared. Now that was most strange. Her cousin Isabella had not mentioned anything about returning to town—quite to the contrary; she appeared to give the impression that she was not often permitted to come into Bath on her own. Uncle William was rather strict about that sort of thing, after... Well.

But there was the name, clearly written in an elegant hand.

Poor Isabella. Joy wondered at times whether she should visit Chalcroft more often, even if it was out of the way. If there was any Fitzroy who would understand how it felt to be left on the shelf, it was Issy.

"There you are."

Joy's heart skipped a beat as a familiar voice spoke behind her. In the fraction of a second before she turned to greet Mr. Gilbert Kitteridge, she tried to control herself.

He is just a gentleman, Joy told herself, swallowing down her panic. *You are seeing him in a public place, and he is not going to kiss you again—he may even regret having kissed you in the first place!* All she had to do was stay calm, and not embarrass herself.

As though that was easy...

Joy turned on the spot to see Gilbert, elegantly dressed in a bottle-green greatcoat that made him seem even more handsome—if that was possible—and with a broad smile on his face.

She smiled weakly. "Pump."

Gilbert's face creased into a frown. "I beg your pardon?"

For goodness' sake, was she going to make a complete fool of herself? Joy almost lifted a hand to her head, she felt so overcome with nerves.

She needed to get a grip on herself if she was not going to

lose any favor she had managed to glean from this gentleman—and that would be much easier if her heart was not frantically beating, preventing her from hearing almost anything, save her own pulse.

"Miss Fitzroy?"

Joy swallowed, then tried weakly to smile. She was being ridiculous. A kiss was only a kiss. True, it had been her first kiss, but it was certainly not Gilbert's—Mr. Kitteridge's. He had two daughters, for pity's sake!

No, if she was going to survive this encounter with her dignity intact, she needed to stay calm and remind herself that matrimony was not on the cards here. This was just a flirtation. And a flirtation, Joy reminded herself, was far more excitement than she had ever got before. She should be grateful. Take whatever flattery Gilbert wished to dole out, and—

"Are you flushing because of me?" Gilbert asked quietly, stepping close.

"No," said Joy automatically, feeling her cheeks flush even more.

Why could she not control a single thing about herself? Why had she even thought coming here would be a good idea, if all she was going to do was look the fool!

But there was no sign of disgust or mockery on Gilbert's face. On the contrary, he smiled and silently offered her his arm.

Joy hesitated only a moment before taking it. Well, she was at the Pump Room, wasn't she? It was perfectly natural for her to take the arm of a gentleman when it was offered to her. She was just like every other lady in the place.

Except that she was walking with the most handsome gentleman in the room.

Joy tried to push away that thought, but it was true. As the two of them started walking slowly around the room, with the flow of the crowd, she could not help but notice that there was not a single other gentleman with half the good looks of Gilbert Kitteridge.

She even espied a rather envious look from Miss Marnion, if she was not mistaken.

"You are flushing," said Gilbert. "I must say, it is good to have that effect on a beautiful woman again."

There was nothing Joy could say—she was too preoccupied attempting not to blush even more. How did he do it? How did he know just what words to say to make her astonished, to embarrass her, to bring out the color of her cheeks?

Thankfully, Joy was left in merciful silence for at least a minute, giving her a chance to absorb just what it felt like to be on his arm once again.

Wonderful. As though…as though she was coming home.

"It appears everyone in Society is here this morning," said Gilbert conversationally, with none of the intensity of his previous words.

"I suppose so, though I would say most are not worth knowing," Joy said instinctively.

She raised her hand to her mouth. Had she really said that? Usually she just thought these things; her family had trained her not to speak them aloud. Even on the rare occasion they slipped from her lips at home, she was subjected to their glares.

"That is not the sort of thing a lady says, Joy Fitzroy," her mother would say sternly.

And now she had said it right here, in public…to Gilbert Kitteridge!

Joy glanced nervously at the man on whose arm she was walking, hunting for clues as to his reaction to her words—but instead of the furrowed brow she expected, Gilbert was…laughing.

"Dear me, Miss Fitzroy, you speak as you find," he said with a chuckle. "I do not think I have ever heard such an acerbic tongue!"

Joy sighed and her shoulders slumped as they reached the end of the room and made their turn. "I know. Many people do not like it, and I have done my best to train it out of me but…well, I speak as I find."

"Good," said Gilbert. "I like it. I like you."

Joy stared up at him. What was he thinking, saying such things to her? Did he not understand what such comments could suggest, could…could lead to? Was Gilbert Kitteridge just a tease, a gentleman who liked to have a lady on his arm, or was this something more? Something real?

And how to goodness was she supposed to find out?

"Look," she said, deciding that directness was the only way. "Why do you say that?"

Gilbert raised an eyebrow. "Say what?"

How was such a handsome man so infuriating? "You know precisely what I mean."

"Do I?"

"Gilbert Kitteridge!"

"I like it when you say my name," he said in a low voice, tightening his grip on her hand. "Say it again."

Joy swallowed, utterly lost for words. Was this what gentlemen said? Was this typical of courting? She had little experience of it, but had spent plenty of years in Society and no one had ever…no man had ever…

A warmth she had only felt with Gilbert was rushing through her body again; her fingers tingled on his arm; her whole body ached for him. What was he doing to her?

"I say such things because they are the truth," Gilbert said, in that low, intimate voice that sent shivers down Joy's spine. "This may not surprise you, Joy, as you know—"

"You should not call me that."

It was scandalous that a man should call her by her first name, and in public…but the trouble was, it felt so natural. So intimate. Joy did not want to hear anyone else say her name for the rest of her life.

Gilbert glanced at her, something fiery and dark in his eyes. "But I want to. As I say, after my wife, I have learnt to say what I feel, when I feel it. You never know when it's too late."

"She died giving birth to my turtle doves. Twins, you know. Very dangerous—they told us that when the doctor suspected it was not one but two babes."

Joy swallowed. Of course. After losing one's spouse so suddenly, one had to take every moment, clutch at it, cling to it, make every moment matter. But that was a life philosophy, not a courting technique!

"That does not mean you need to say that I-I am beautiful," she said in a whisper, hoping that no one was paying attention to them. "And things like that."

Gilbert chuckled. "Why not? It is true, and it gives me pleasure, and I hope it would give you a little pleasure. I would like to give you pleasure, Joy."

Joy stopped in her tracks.

He could not say such things! And yet she wanted him to say such things, wanted him to mean them. Wanted him to kiss her again, to let her taste the passion of a person, something she had never done before she met Gilbert.

Because he had walked into her life, with his two turtle doves, and made her feel…

Murmurs were sparking up around them. Joy flushed, suddenly conscious that she was attracting the attention of people in the Pump Room. One person was even pointing a finger!

"Joy?" murmured Gilbert.

He had still not let go of her arm, and Joy did not want him to. Did not want to lose this connection, something so precious, so new…but how could she in all decency continue walking with him, with him saying such things?

"It gives me pleasure, and I hope it would give you a little pleasure. I would like to give you pleasure, Joy."

"What do you want from me?" she breathed.

Gilbert appeared to hesitate for a moment before replying, and when he did, Joy could do nothing but look into his eyes and hope it was all true. "Want from you? Everything. Everything you want to give me, everything about yourself you have hidden from the world. All those parts of you the world told you were not enough, not important, not perfect… I want to see them, Joy, and glory in them. I want you to see yourself as I see you."

Joy's jaw dropped. He was mad. That was not the sort of thing a gentleman said to a lady, particularly not in public!

Yet they were precisely the words she had longed to hear, even though she had not known it for so long. His touch revived her soul, his kiss captured her entirely, and how he was saying such things?

"You cannot mean that," she said.

A wicked look flashed across Gilbert's face, but it was gone in an instant. "Don't tell me what I don't mean, Joy Fitzroy, for I would have great pleasure in showing you just how much I want you."

Joy held his gaze for a moment, mouth still open, unable to take in the intensity of his words—and then it was over.

Gilbert faced forward again and started slowly promenading around the Pump Room, and Joy was pulled inexorably along with him, her hand still in the crook of his arm.

It was a wonder she was able to walk. Joy was not sure how she was still standing. Her heart was racing so frantically that she felt it could burst from her chest at any moment. Her lungs just about remembered how to breathe, and there was such desire in her, desire she had never known before, but now that it had risen, what was she going to do about it?

"They are still staring," she said.

A prickle of discomfort curled around her heart. It was never pleasant being stared at, and as she had grown older, Joy had become the example mamas gave to their daughters at balls. She had even heard one of them, once. *"Smile, for goodness' sake, or you'll end up like Miss Fitzroy!"*

But Gilbert merely laughed. "So they are."

"I wish they would not," Joy admitted in a low voice.

"Why?" he said as they reached the end of the room and turned. "They are merely trying to understand why a beauty like you is here, walking with a gentleman like me."

Joy glanced up at Gilbert. He honestly seemed to believe the words he was saying. It was unaccountable. How did a gentleman like that, looking like that, as good and kind as Harmony had described him, decide that she was the sort of lady he wished to accompany?

"You do not have to lie to me, you know," she said. "I am perfectly at peace with my appearance, and my position in Society."

Gilbert stopped dead in his tracks. When he turned to look at Joy, there was an expression of genuine confusion on his face.

"Joy Fitzroy," he said in wonder, "you do not know how attractive you are, do you?"

Joy flushed, dropping her gaze to the floor. Why did he say such things? Was it for his own amusement? Surely not. He would not have sought her company if he was merely to tease her; he was her sister's neighbor, after all, and he was well aware that she was not unprotected.

So why, then?

"I think you are teasing me, sir," she said, looking up into Gilbert's eyes.

There was that wicked expression in them once again. "In that case, Miss Joy Fitzroy, I will make it my mission to make you believe it."

CHAPTER SIX

JOY WAS ABSOLUTELY not going to take the waters, because she might see Gilbert there.

Absolutely not.

That would be foolish, she told herself as the December wind whipped at her skirts and she pulled her pelisse tight around a scarf to keep out the cold. *And it would be wanton.* Ladies should not go around Bath hunting down gentlemen.

The thought made her smile, but it was swiftly removed when Joy noticed a pair of gentlemen looking at her—not just looking, but pointing.

Holding her head up high as best she could, Joy tried to walk past them, but—

"Hi there! Are you not Miss Fitzroy?"

Joy hesitated. It would be terribly bad manners to continue walking without addressing the gentleman who had spoken to her—who had not only spoken to her, but appeared to know her. His face was unfamiliar to her, but that was by the by. Most gentlemen looked the same.

Except for Gilbert.

Pushing aside the thought of the gentleman on her heart, Joy said stiffly, "Yes. And you are?"

The gentleman grinned. "I heard about you! Oldest spinster in Bath, they say!"

His companion chuckled, and Joy's cheeks warmed. Drawing herself up as best she could, she stalked away, ignoring the peals of laughter that followed her.

Oldest spinster in Bath, indeed! There were plenty of ladies older than her and unmarried—oh, if only a woman's marital status did not matter... After all, one's place in Society was almost entirely dictated by one's husband and one's father. Hers would not live forever, and without a husband...

She turned a corner and saw something that made her heart freeze and her feet still.

Gilbert Kitteridge.

There he was, in the abbey churchyard. She had been right, or at least, partially right. He was here, though not to taste the waters. Paloma and Jemmy were dancing around him, laughing as they scared the pigeons into the air; wings flapping and disgruntled squawks filled the place. But it was not the only sound.

A woman's laugh, musical and light, accompanied the children.

Joy swiftly stepped to the side, hiding behind one of the pillars outside the Pump Room as dread sank into her stomach like a stone.

There were the girls, running around, their breath blossoming out into the freezing air.

There was Gilbert, watching them and laughing, shaking his head as the pigeons immediately settled back down on the pavement, utterly unimpressed by the girls' efforts.

And there...

Joy swallowed. There was a woman, probably four or five years younger than her, dressed in a most elegant pelisse, which matched her bonnet, laughing along with them.

She should have known.

A rush of despair accompanied the dread that had already settled in her stomach, weighing her down and making it impossible to think of anything but betrayal.

Betrayal. It was a harsh thing to think, but Joy could consider no other word suitable for such a wrenching sight. What had Gilbert told her only the day before?

"In that case, Miss Joy Fitzroy, I will make it my mission to make you believe it."

And she had believed him, too. That was the most depressing part of the whole situation. Joy had believed him, looking into those impressive eyes, that handsome face, and she had wanted so desperately to believe this was her moment, one that she would never forget.

She would never forget it now, but for quite different reasons.

"Careful, Paloma!" The woman giggled, reaching out for the little girl just as she was about to tip over. "There we go—go get that one!"

The child laughed raucously as though she had not been about to split her head on the pavement, and Gilbert shot the woman a grateful look.

It was perhaps that which hurt the most. Oh, Joy knew the entire situation was a disaster, one that she would ruminate on a great deal, but it was Gilbert's easy way with this woman, whoever she was, his gratitude to her for helping with his children.

"In that case, Miss Joy Fitzroy, I will make it my mission to make you believe it."

It was all lies. She could not trust him; she could not believe a word he said. Just when she was starting to wonder whether she truly was as pretty as he was making out...

What a fool she was.

"Watch me, watch me, Maggie!"

Joy's heart twisted. Perhaps Gilbert and his children were on first-name terms with all the ladies in his life, though goodness knew how many there were.

Oh, she had been so easily led, even to the point where she had wondered...

"I found someone."

Joy tightened her jaw. She was ignorant no longer. She knew what Gilbert was, a cad, a rake, and she could take precautions now to protect her heart. And the first thing she needed to do, before she was spotted, was escape this nightmare.

Escaping, however, quickly proved to be impossible.

"Miss Fitzroy! Miss Fitzroy, is that you?"

Joy froze in her attempt to leave, back turned, but she knew Gilbert's voice anywhere.

"It *is* you!"

Arranging her face into a frosty, cold expression, Joy turned around and tried her best to keep her head up high as she said, "Yes? Oh, Mr. Kitteridge. I did not see you there."

"Look at me, Joy!" screamed Jemmy, rather making it impossible for Joy's protestation that she had not seen the Kitteridge family to be true.

"Come on over," said Gilbert, waving at her. "Meet Miss Maggie!"

Joy swallowed. All she had to do was say that she had a prior engagement; no one would know, and it was a perfectly reasonable excuse. It would also save her the bother of having her heart entirely broken by her being forced to meet this young woman who was so evidently a close part of the Kitteridge family. As she had wished to be.

She pushed the thought from her mind. No, she was not going to let Gilbert—Mr. Kitteridge know just how much he had injured her. She was a Fitzroy. No one injured a Fitzroy.

"I did not mean to intrude," Joy said as she stepped across the square to where Gilbert and Miss Maggie were standing.

"Oh, no intrusion, please," said the woman pleasantly.

Joy scowled at her. *Well, how dare she be so—so polite and welcoming!*

"No, you're not intruding," said Gilbert easily. "In fact, I would say it is even better now you are here. Wouldn't you say, my turtle doves?"

His daughters giggled. One, Joy was not sure which, said,

"We're not turtle doves!"

"Of course you are!" Gilbert said, a teasing look on his face. "Otherwise, why would I be about to eat you?"

Spreading out his arms like an eagle, Gilbert dropped his head and rushed toward his daughters, who screamed with laughter and ran around the square, attempting to evade him.

Miss Maggie giggled as she shook her head wryly, and Joy smiled weakly. Well, this was a perfect family scene. But it was not her family, and it never would be. Not with such a woman beside her.

Joy stole a glance at her. Yes, she had been right when she espied her from across the square. Pretty, young, well dressed. Everything a gentleman would want in a partner.

Everything she was not.

She looked down at her pelisse. It had seen better days. There had been no point in replacing it, not when it could be mended...but now she stood beside Miss Maggie, Joy was horribly conscious of just how much darning had been put into her hems.

"Now," said Gilbert, huffing and puffing as he returned to the ladies' side. "My turtle doves will be going adventuring with Miss Maggie. Bear hunting."

Joy blinked. She surely could not have heard that correctly. "I beg your pardon?"

"Bear hunting," repeated Gilbert, as though it was the most natural thing in the world.

Joy looked between Miss Maggie and Gilbert, attempting to decipher the puzzle.

"We're going bear hunting, Joy!" said one of the twins, grabbing her hand and grinning. "Are you coming with us?"

"Sadly not," Gilbert said before Joy could say anything. "Joy is coming with me."

Joy looked up from the child to Gilbert, and tried her best to give him a stony glare. It did not appear to work. The man just grinned, as though he had created the best plan anyone could ever have hoped for.

Then he looked at the woman beside her. "Are you ready?"

"Ready as I will ever be, Gilbert," said Miss Maggie with a wink.

Joy looked away, heat flushing across her chest. Well, really! Such intimacy was hardly to be expected between a husband and wife in public, let alone between two people who were not married!

How dare he! After all the things he'd said to her, all those moments…

"Don't tell me what I don't mean, Joy Fitzroy, for I would have great pleasure in showing you just how much I want you."

"Apparently there are bears in Bath, so we are on a mission to catch them," said Miss Maggie, winking at Joy.

Joy stared at her, open-mouthed. Was there no end to the audacity?

Miss Maggie glanced nervously at Gilbert, as though it was Joy's behavior that was outrageous, and not her own. "Right. Well, Gilbert, we will see you later."

After dropping a light curtsey—short of what was expected by formality, Joy thought irritably, but considering the lack of distance between them, entirely expected—Miss Maggie took the hands of the two girls.

"Come on, turtle doves," she said brightly. "Where do you think the bears will be?"

"Sydney Gardens!" one of them said as they wandered off.

Joy watched Gilbert as his daughters disappeared from the square. There was a look of rather uncertain contentment on his face, as though he knew his daughters were happy, but he was not.

Well, Joy had had just about enough of this family. Gilbert could say she was coming with him all he wanted, but she had better things to do than make a fool out of herself. She had not known it before, but she knew now. It was time to leave.

"How pleasant to see you, Mr. Kitteridge," Joy said formally, dropping into what she considered was a much more appropriate curtsey, then rising to say, "I must be going, but—"

"It's strange, seeing them together."

Joy stared. Gilbert's words were so odd that she hardly knew what to say. "I-I…I beg your pardon?"

"Maggie and the girls," said Gilbert, sighing. "You think you are prepared, then…"

His voice trailed away.

Joy swallowed. She did not wish to hear from Gilbert how strange it was to see his future wife with his children. That was a conversation she could certainly do without!

"You must excuse me," she said, and stepped away.

At least, she attempted to step away. For some reason, there was a hand on her arm.

"Joy," said Gilbert softly. "What's wrong?"

Despite her desire to escape, a part of Joy forced her to remain, turning slowly on the spot to look up into Gilbert's concerned eyes.

How did he do that, look at her as though *she* was being strange in her behavior? Joy felt anger rise in her chest at the injustice of it all. She was not the one whispering words of affection to one woman, speaking to another by her first name, and sending off his children with her! Who knew how many ladies he was speaking to in that fashion?

"I did not wish to intrude, as I said," Joy said stiffly, wrenching her arm from his grip. "I wish you every happiness."

She had almost managed to reach the pillars of the Pump Room when Gilbert caught up with her again, this time moving to block her path.

"Every happiness?" he repeated, confusion on his face. "What are you talking about?"

"Your Miss Maggie!" said Joy, pointing in the direction the three of them had gone, hating that he could so easily see her upset. "Why would you talk to me about—about pleasure, and kisses, and…"

Her voice trailed away; she was conscious she was speaking

loudly enough for others to hear.

She swallowed. She had to say this, had to get it out. She would not permit herself to be walked over like a wallflower.

"I would prefer it if you do not speak to me again," Joy said coldly. "As I said, I wish you every happiness with Miss Maggie."

Gilbert looked absolutely delighted. Joy glared up at him, unable to see what was so marvelous. Did he not understand her?

"Joy Fitzroy, you are such a woman as I had never imagined," he said.

Joy's hackles rose. "How are you—"

"Maggie is my governess."

Joy stared. *Governess?*

"Technically I suppose she is my sister-in-law, first and foremost. She came to help me when the girls were born, and now she looks after them three afternoons a week," said Gilbert, that same silly grin on his face. "I must say, she is more a part of the family now than I had realized. I suppose I do speak to her with a certain irreverence—something I will have to cease when she marries her sweetheart in the New Year."

Joy's mouth fell open. She closed it again hurriedly, opened it in an attempt to speak, then closed it again.

Sister-in-law. Governess.

Embarrassment was not the word. There was not a word for how foolish she felt. The freezing Christmas air was unable to penetrate her as she stood in abject misery.

"Ah," she said weakly.

Gilbert shook his head. "Ah indeed. Joy Fitzroy, you were jealous!"

"I was not jealous," Joy lied instinctively.

"You were jealous, and I am glad," he said. "Goodness, I am not entirely sure what that says about me, but there we go. Come on."

Without his waiting for her to acquiesce, Joy found herself walking arm in arm with Gilbert.

Well, she had made a fool of herself and no mistake, she

thought darkly. Why had she not thought of that? Why had she just assumed… But she knew full well why. A strange sort of protective, jealous instinct had overtaken her, and she had seen Gilbert as…well, *hers*.

Something to protect. Something to guard covetously.

"I…I suppose I need to apologize—Gilbert!"

Joy had not intended to shout his name, but she was much provoked. Just as she had settled herself into a calm walking pace, summoning up the courage to admit she had been at fault, Gilbert suddenly pulled her into a dark, dank alleyway.

Looking around herself frantically, Joy could not see why he had done such a thing—but then Gilbert pushed her against the wall and covered her chest with his own.

"Joy Fitzroy," he muttered, "you do something to me—something you do not even realize."

Joy gasped, hardly able to take in the sudden change. They were here alone, where no one would ever come upon them… They could do anything…

"I might kiss you, you know," said Gilbert in a low voice, his eyes darting from her own to her lips then back again.

Joy swallowed, licking her lips, and he groaned. "I might want you to."

She had not considered such words—they had just poured out of her—but they felt right. The reaction they sparked in Gilbert, however, proved that they were definitely right.

He lowered his head, just inches above her lips. "And if I did?"

Joy attempted to think, but it was impossible. All rational thought had left her mind, leaving only desire and a desperate need to do, to feel, to be as close to Gilbert as possible.

This was scandalous, simply not done…and she wanted to do it. Very badly.

"If you did," she breathed, feeling the delightful way his chest pressed up against hers, reveling in the enclosed feeling he created, "then I would…would…"

She had never had this sort of conversation before—had

never expected to. *What sort of things do lovers say to each other?* Joy wondered, heart racing. How could she say the sort of things that were in her mind?

"I would kiss you in return," Joy said, hardly daring to believe she was saying these things. "I would pull you toward me, and cling to you, and I would want…want…"

She could not continue. It was rather difficult to think now that Gilbert's lips were delicately grazing her neck with kisses she could only just feel.

Joy arched her back against the wall, trying to push herself closer to him, to feel the kisses scalding down her neck, but Gilbert moved away, and she moaned in desperate need.

"Damn, Joy," Gilbert whispered. "The things I could do to you here…"

Joy moaned again, unable to help herself. Desperate anticipation was tingling across her entire body, and she needed him in a way she had never known before.

If Gilbert Kitteridge did not kiss her soon, she would be forced to do something very reckless.

Like kiss him herself.

"But I shouldn't."

Joy gasped. The sudden absence of Gilbert, now that he had stepped away and was leaning against the opposite alley wall, panting as though he had run a marathon, was startling in its emptiness.

She needed him. Didn't he see that? Didn't he know?

"Shouldn't?"

Gilbert shook his head, never for a moment taking his eyes from her. "I shouldn't, Joy. I am a widower, so there is no stain on *my* reputation if I form a dalliance with anyone, but you…your reputation is intact. Precious. It should not be risked."

Joy blinked. Not be risked?

"You are mistaken," she said, boldness seeping in where fear had once been. "My reputation does nothing but keep me aloof from the world, and I do not want—I want you, Gilbert. I would rather have you than a reputation."

A shadow passed over Gilbert's eyes, and then he was kissing her, pushing her against the wall in his ardor, and Joy clung to him, desperate for him, her hands around his neck and her leg raised against his hip.

She wanted him, wanted all of him, wanted to encircle him and enclose him and be encircled by him. His lips were rough against hers, his tongue demanding, and she allowed him in, pleasure sparking across her body. His hands at her waist held her tight so she could not escape…

As if she ever would wish to.

Joy gave herself up to the pleasure, knew this desire within her had to be unleashed, and moaned as Gilbert's hand moved up to her breast under her pelisse.

New pleasures, new sensations soared through her. How could one person take such pleasure?

CHAPTER SEVEN

"NO, REALLY, I should leave," said Joy wistfully.

It was strange. Normally, she would be looking for any excuse to leave Harmony's home after being here a full hour.

It was not that the two sisters did not get along, as such. They were just so different, had been since they were children. Joy had come to accept that, knowing that sisterhood was a coincidence of fate. But these last few days…

They had been getting along better than ever.

Joy took another sip of tea and sighed happily in the armchair in Harmony's drawing room. Their conversation had flowed, there had been no awkward silences, and, best of all, she had said nothing to upset nor offend her sister.

It was a miracle.

"Oh, you can stay," said Harmony comfortably, glancing at a clock. "Besides, it is not as though you have anywhere to be."

Joy's smile faltered slightly. It was the truth, after all. She could not fault her for that.

"Thank you," she said as graciously as she could manage. "That is very kind."

"Another biscuit?"

Joy gratefully took another of the delightful biscuits that her sister's cook made almost every day—a real treat—and settled back into the armchair.

Yes, it was remarkably pleasant here at Harmony's home, and Joy's presence here was absolutely nothing to do with her neighbor.

Joy's smile was accompanied by a flushing of her cheeks. Gilbert Kitteridge. No, she was not here to see him, she told herself—she was here to see her sister, Harmony. Any hopes she had of perhaps seeing him leave the house were absolute nonsense.

"My reputation does nothing but keep me aloof from the world, and I do not want—I want you, Gilbert. I would rather have you than a reputation."

A rush of heat that had nothing to do with the tea she was drinking seared Joy's chest. Just a few hours ago she had been pressed up against a wall having her breasts fondled and her mouth ravished…

"Joy?"

Joy started and flushed.

Her sister was looking at her closely. "Are you quite well? You look a little warm—you are too close to the fire."

"I am perfectly well," said Joy hastily. Lord, the idea that Harmony could perhaps infer what she was thinking merely by her expression… "Just thinking, that is all."

"Thinking?"

Too late, Joy wished she had kept her mouth shut. Harmony was not nosey—not like their cousin Lucy, or Olivia—but she was no fool.

"You know, you are…different," Harmony said delicately.

Joy tried to fight back her instinct—to roundly defend herself by saying there was absolutely nothing different about her, and why would anyone wish there to be—and smiled weakly. "Oh?"

Harmony nodded, taking a sip of her own tea before continuing, "It's a recent change, I must say. The last few days or so. You seem…happier. More content in yourself."

"More joyful," Joy said wryly.

Her sister grinned. "Well, I suppose so. What's happened?

What's different?"

Joy hoped that her sister's husband would come back into the drawing room and distract them. She could taste the panic in her mouth, accompanied by the bitter memory of the tea.

Gilbert Kitteridge.

That was what was different. Joy knew it; that was the only difference in her life, though it was difficult to believe it had only been four days since she first met him.

Her entire life seemed to be full of Gilbert, though he was a very recent acquaintance. Yet what an impact he had had on her life.

"You are beautiful."

Joy smiled weakly. "Oh, you know. Excited for Christmas."

It was a pathetic excuse, to her mind, but Harmony swallowed it up quite happily.

"Oh, yes, I long to see Chalcroft again—you know, I do not believe I have seen it since the summer! And what a beautiful place it is, so charming. I hope Rufus will be big enough to feed the geese this year. Remember last year? He was so small…"

Joy nodded and smiled at all the right moments as Harmony launched into reminiscences of her son at Chalcroft Farm. It left Joy to think about a rather charming individual who simply would not leave her mind alone.

Gilbert Kitteridge. She had embarrassed herself, certainly, by thinking his sister-in-law was his betrothed—or worse, his paramour—but in a way, the misunderstanding had brought them closer.

A clock chimed, and Joy turned to see, to her surprise, that it was nearly six o'clock.

"My goodness, I should go," she said hastily, placing down her teacup and rising to her feet. "Our parents will be wondering—"

"Oh, I sent a note around that you were staying for dinner here," said David quietly as he stepped into the room.

Joy stared at her brother-in-law. *Well, the presumption!* "I beg your pardon?"

"Oh, David, what a wonderful idea," said Harmony, clapping her hands together. "It'll be the four of us, then?"

Joy turned from David to Harmony. "Four of us?"

"Well, I have a friend coming to dinner, and I thought it would be nice to have four," said David easily as he sat beside his wife and indicated that Joy too should be seated.

Joy remained on her feet. "A friend?"

"Oh, an even number is so much more pleasant around a dining table," said Harmony, smiling besottedly at her husband. "You are so clever."

"Not as clever as you," said David.

Joy looked away as her sister kissed her husband. Well, it was a fait accompli, and very well done. A friend, eh? If she was not very much mistaken, one or both of her parents had asked her sister to introduce Joy to a gentleman with the desperate hope of marrying her off…and this was the result.

Dinner with Harmony, and David…and David's friend.

"Joy?"

Joy glanced back at her sister. There was a genuine look of excitement on Harmony's face, and it would not be Joy who removed it.

That was the trouble with her sister. She was so…so good. So lovely. It was difficult to deny her anything.

Joy slowly lowered herself back into the armchair with a weak smile. "A friend of David's. How wonderful."

Harmony nodded and started chattering on about her hopes for Rufus' friends when he was grown, but Joy was hardly listening. A desperate hope had entered her heart, and even though she knew it was impossible, entirely impossible, it would not disappear.

Could the friend…could David's friend possibly be Gilbert?

No. Joy pushed the thought from her mind as decidedly as she could. Surely if their dinner guest was Gilbert, they would have said as much; Harmony had been there with the two of them, so she knew they were acquainted. Besides, would they not say "our neighbor" rather than "David's friend"?

The doorbell rang.

"Oh, and there he is now," said Harmony with a smile, rising to her feet to greet their guest. "I hope you do not mind, Joy, but I decided to invite—"

"Gilbert," said Joy weakly.

Gilbert grinned as the maid welcomed him into the drawing room. "My word, Joy! What a surprise!"

Joy looked wordlessly between the three of them, but was unable to decipher their expressions. *Was* it a surprise? Or was this all some strange sort of conspiracy between them? Surely…surely her sister would not have done such a thing if she knew what Joy and Gilbert had been sharing in an alley that morning…

"You look a little warm again, Joy," said Harmony, before she curtseyed to Gilbert then indicated he should be seated.

Joy laughed weakly as she half sat, half fell into the armchair. A little warm?

How she managed to get through an hour of light conversation, she did not know. Harmony was chatty, helping guide the conversation along many interesting paths that did not require Joy to contribute.

How could she, conscious as she was of Gilbert's presence?

It was only when the four of them went through to the intimate dining room and she saw Gilbert was seated beside her that Joy had a moment to speak to him privately.

"You did not think to bring your turtle doves?"

Gilbert grinned as he murmured, "If I could get you on my own, I would."

Joy's cheeks flushed as Harmony spoke to her maid.

The way he spoke to her…it were as though they were alone, not seated opposite her sister and her husband!

For a moment, Joy was overcome with a strange sensation. This was what it would be like if she and Gilbert… Well.

Harmony and her husband, Joy and her own. The four of them would perhaps dine together once a week—more often when the children were older.

She tried her best to put the intriguing idea out of her mind. That was something she could ponder in the privacy of her own bedchamber that evening. At least for now, she would have to attempt to survive a dinner with Gilbert…with the audience of her sister.

The trouble was, Gilbert did not appear to care very much that they were technically in company. Charming and witty, he nevertheless was somehow able, while Harmony and David talked between themselves, to…

Joy could not think of another word for it. *Flirt* with her.

"So tell me," Gilbert said softly as he poured wine into her glass, "did you purposely stay late at your sister's so they had no choice but to invite you to dinner, all in an attempt to see me?"

Joy's stomach fluttered. "What would you do if I had?"

Gilbert's smile broadened as he placed the wine bottle down. "Let me show you."

Without taking his eyes from hers, calmly and naturally, as though this was perfectly normal, he removed his hand from the table, took hers, and moved it to his thigh.

At least, Joy thought he was moving it to his thigh. But he kept going. Inch by inch, slowly but surely, Gilbert placed her hand on his erect manhood pulsing under his breeches.

Joy's gasp was hidden by a particularly loud burst of laughter from her sister at something her husband said. How could this be happening?

His manhood twitched as her lips parted, and Gilbert grinned wickedly. "That is what I would do to you."

Joy swallowed, but did not pull her hand away. It was outrageous. It was more sensual than she could imagine—and she wanted more. It was difficult to believe he could be so bold!

"Do you not think, Kitteridge?"

Gilbert broke their gaze and smiled as he released Joy's hand.

"Oh, I quite agree."

Joy's breath was caught in her throat. How had he… Why did he think he could…

But he had. And the worst of it all was that she had enjoyed it. Enjoyed touching him, feeling the very physical evidence of his desire—desire that had to be for her, was it not?

Before she knew it, the dinner was over. Her pudding sat there, almost untouched, and her mind was entirely lost in thoughts of Gilbert as a maid picked it up and took it away.

"Well, I think we ladies will retire," said Harmony with a wry smile. "Give you gentlemen an excuse to talk about all the dull topics you have avoided at the table."

Gilbert chuckled. "Goodness, you know me well. Thank you, Mrs. Navarre."

The two gentlemen rose, and so did Harmony. All three of them looked at Joy, though she could not understand why.

"Joy?" said Harmony, raising her eyebrows.

Joy stared blankly up at her. "Yes? Oh, yes, right."

She rose hastily and was forced to steady her chair to prevent it from tipping over. Really, she needed to get a hold of herself. She could not permit this nonsense to continue!

Gilbert Kitteridge was a tease, certainly, and he desired her. Well, she desired him.

But that was as far as it went, Joy told herself as she and Harmony stepped back into the drawing room. It was not as though anything was going to happen!

"Joy Fitzroy, you tell me the truth right this moment," Harmony said, sitting firmly down and glaring up at her older sister.

Joy swallowed. "What?" She had not intended to sound so defensive as she sat beside her sister on the sofa.

"You and Gilbert Kitteridge, that's what," said Harmony with a small smile. "Do not think I did not see the two of you."

Joy's cheeks turned warm. Had Harmony—

"Making eyes at each other at the table, speaking so intimately. I have never known you to be so comfortable in the presence of a gentleman!" said Harmony. "Except David, of course, and Papa, but they do not count. Is he courting you? Has he asked for your hand? Have you kissed him?"

"Harmony!"

Her sister shrugged. "Well, I am an old married woman now, Joy," she said with a teasing air. "I have to know these things."

Absolutely not, thought Joy darkly. The day she told Harmony the sorts of things she and Gilbert had... Well, it was not even to be thought of.

"He has not asked for my hand," she said.

Harmony waited, then nudged her. "And?"

"And I do not know what more I can tell you!" Joy said with a weak laugh. "Is Gilbert Kitteridge courting me? I do not think so, but I cannot pretend he and I have not...are not... I enjoy his company."

It was but a tenth of what she felt about him, in truth, but Joy was not about to admit all that to her sister...not with Gilbert in the next room.

Perhaps he was receiving just such a grilling from David, she thought wryly. Perhaps she should have warned him that Harmony, though quiet, was sharp.

"Joy Fitzroy, tell me everything!"

"No," said Joy shortly.

Harmony's eyes widened, but not in upset, but curiosity. "You...you truly like him, don't you?"

Joy hesitated, but surely there could be no danger in admitting that...could there? "Yes. I like him."

"Should my ears be burning?"

Joy turned quickly to see the gentlemen returning to the drawing room. There was a wide smile on Gilbert's face. Of course he would return just as she said that!

"No," she said with a sweet smile, "I was speaking of someone more pleasant than you."

"Gilbert, may I offer you a drink?" said Harmony, rising swiftly and indicating he should be seated on the sofa. "David, if you would not mind…"

Joy had to admit, it was expertly done. Gilbert was now seated beside her on the sofa while her sister and her husband were on the other side of the room, speaking loudly about the state of brandy these days.

She smiled ruefully. "I believe my sister has ulterior motives on your person."

Gilbert grinned mischievously. "Goodness, I am not sure I would like to come between your sister and David Navarre."

"Not in that way!" Joy said with a laugh. Truly, the idea of Harmony with anyone save David was out of the question. "Where are the turtle doves this evening?"

"At our house in the country for a few days, with my parents," said Gilbert. "I will join them for Christmas. We are so rarely in town, and the girls much prefer being with their grandparents. I would be offended, if I was not so charmed."

Joy's smile fell a little at his words. So Gilbert would not be in Bath much longer. This…this whatever it was, for she was not entirely sure, would be over before it begun.

That was why she did not know him, had never made his acquaintance before; that was why she had not met him on one of her numerous visits to her sister.

They did not actually live in Bath. The Kitteridge family was only here for a short time, clearly, and would soon be disappearing from the town, and from her life. He would be gone, taking all her hopes with him.

"Is that a frown on my behalf?"

"No," said Joy reflexively, and then laughed weakly. "Maybe."

She had always had that habit, of protecting herself without thinking, but something about Gilbert was changing that.

His smile was a little too knowing, however. "I am honored."

"Yes," said Joy dryly. "I believe you are the only one in that regard. Few people enjoy my frowns."

"Then I am even more honored," said Gilbert softly. "A

frown from you is far more precious than a smile from anyone else."

Joy swallowed. Gilbert had, at some point in their conversation—she could not entirely tell when—taken her hands in his. It was a good thing Harmony and David were still extolling the virtues of French brandy on the other side of the room, for if they saw her now…

"You probably shouldn't hold my hands," she said, not looking away from his eyes. "Here, I mean."

"I probably should not have kissed you in that alley earlier today," said Gilbert. "But I am very glad I did."

Her heart was doing that thing again: beating too quickly, then skipping a beat entirely. Joy did not like it; it felt out of control, wild, and yet she would not wish to leave this moment for—

"But sadly I must depart," said Gilbert, releasing her hands and rising to his feet in one smooth motion. "I cannot trespass on your sister's hospitality any longer."

"Oh, you can," said Harmony hurriedly, rushing over. "Truly, Mr. Kitteridge—"

"I should leave as well," said Joy, disappointment at the loss of Gilbert's company rushing through her. What was the point of staying if Gilbert was not? "I'll walk. It's not far."

"Oh, but—"

"I'll take you in my carriage," said Gilbert quickly. "Come on, Miss Fitzroy."

Joy barely had enough time to grab her pelisse before he had bundled her out of the door and into the freezing air.

"David could have walked me home, you know," she said pointedly.

Gilbert's eyes had a rather strange look in them, and when he spoke, temptation flickered across Joy's heart. "Or you could come over to my house. For a nightcap."

Joy stared at Gilbert as she considered his invitation.

She was not so innocent to believe it was for a nightcap. This was an invitation of an entirely different kind, she knew…and she wanted it. Wanted him. Wanted to give in to these desires that had risen within her at his presence.

"That…that sounds lovely," Joy said, reaching out and taking Gilbert's hand. "Yes."

CHAPTER EIGHT

WITH EVERY STEP, Joy wondered whether she should flee.

Not flee, precisely. That suggested she was unwilling to follow Gilbert into his home, and Joy could not be further from unwilling.

"David could have walked me home, you know."

"Or you could come over to my house. For a nightcap."

No, she could not have been more eager to enter a building, with Gilbert's comforting presence just before her as they stepped into the quiet and dark hall. It was just as she had remembered it, though there was no maid to take her things, no shrieks from his girls in the drawing room. The entire place was quiet.

"Empty," said Gilbert, removing his hat and placing it on a console table by the door. "I sent the servants away with the girls. I can make do without them for a few days."

Joy swallowed. *Alone.* Had she ever been truly alone with a gentleman? Not like this, certainly. No one here to watch them, to accidentally come across them, to be scandalized by their time alone together…

"I can make do without them for a few days."

The reality of Gilbert's sentence sank into Joy's heart like a lead weight. A few days—that was all she had with him, then he would be gone. Back to the country, to his daughters, to his life— a life without her.

She would never see him again.

Though the thought brought a certain amount of misery to Joy's heart, it also created a flicker of excitement.

Whatever happened this evening—and she was still not sure what she wanted to happen—it would not matter. Gilbert was not going to remain in town and would not tell anyone, she was sure. He would just disappear into the night. A Christmas she would never forget…but one that no one else would ever have to remember.

A shiver of anticipation rushed through her. She could do anything, be anyone, kiss Gilbert as much as she wanted, and the world would never know. Her reputation would be safe.

"Joy?"

Joy swallowed. She had just been standing there, like a fool, doing and saying nothing as Gilbert examined her. "Yes? Yes."

Clumsily, she removed her pelisse and handed it to him, and their fingertips brushed ever so gently. Heat, fierce and fiery, rushed through her, and Joy almost dropped the pelisse before Gilbert could take it.

Her gaze met his, and in that moment, she was certain he understood what she had felt. Was it possible he felt it too? The strange desire to be closer, the inexorable feeling that this was leading to something neither of them could fight?

"I do not believe I have ever been invited into a gentleman's home," Joy said weakly as Gilbert opened the drawing room door and beckoned her inside. "Alone, I mean."

The remnants of a fire still smoldered in the grate, and Joy took a seat on the sofa beside it, finding to her surprise she was in absolutely no need of further warmth. There was more than enough fire within her already.

"Really?" Gilbert raised an eyebrow as he sat beside her—far too close to be appropriate, Joy could not help but thinking. Not that she was complaining.

She nodded, finding her mouth rather dry. "The closest I have got, I suppose, was when I acted as chaperone for… I mean… Miss Chesworth and I…"

Joy's voice trailed away as embarrassment flourished in her chest.

Why on earth had she mentioned that? The last thing she should do was point out to Gilbert just how old she was, how outside matrimonial pursuits Society considered her to be.

A chaperone? Why did she have to paint herself into such a dark and dull corner?

But for some reason, the gentleman beside her was smiling. "In truth, I cannot imagine you as a chaperone, Joy. You are too full of life, too witty—too sarcastic by half."

Joy had to laugh. "Oh dear, you know me very well."

"Not nearly as well as I would like," said Gilbert softly.

She swallowed at his words, dropping her gaze to her hands in her lap. How did he do it? Speak that way, as though she was the most interesting woman in the world? Look at her as though he could not drag his eyes away?

It was inexplicable, yet Joy did not want it explained. Then the magic would be gone, the magic of an evening she never thought she would have. Oh, if only he leaned forward and kissed her…that would be the perfect end to the day.

But Joy wanted more than kisses; wild, untamed images arose in her mind, as they sometimes did when presented with a handsome gentleman. But this was not vague pretending about a gentleman she had never been introduced to—she had kissed Gilbert Kitteridge, been kissed by him, knew how he tasted, knew she wanted more.

More, and more than more. More than was appropriate. More than Joy could bear.

And if not now, when? She would never have this chance again, of that she was certain, and there was so much she had never explored, never shared.

Joy's gaze flickered away from her hands to Gilbert's. Did she have enough bravery to simply reach out and take them? What would he do if she did? What would she do if Gilbert pulled away from her?

She did not think she would be able to bear the shame…

"You know, this is something I would never countenance when I was younger."

Joy's attention was lifted from her hands to his teasingly smiling face. "I beg your pardon?"

"This," he said, spreading out his arms and then just happening to place one down on the back of the sofa—a mere inch away from Joy's neck. "Have a lady in my home, just the two of us. I like it. I like you."

Joy's heart twisted slightly as it skipped a beat, but she resolved not to let herself get overwhelmed. She was not for overwhelming.

"I suppose that is one of the characteristics of being a widower," she said as lightly as she could manage. "I mean, there are certain things widows and widowers can do which Society would not permit to others."

Gilbert raised his eyebrows. "Such as?"

"Well…" said Joy hesitantly. What she wished to say, the words dancing across her mind, was far too scandalous to say aloud. "You can…"

Her voice trailed into the silence and her cheeks burned. She should never have brought up the topic if she was not willing to speak her heart!

But all the boldness and bravery, even the brashness Joy was certain she was known for both in her family and in Society, had utterly failed her. Here she was, with a real chance of lovemaking with a gentleman who certainly knew what he was doing, and she could not even speak of such things!

"I can blame things on my children," said Gilbert softly. "No one would ever think to question it."

"Yes, yes, that is the sort of thing I mean, precisely," Joy said, grasping on to his words desperately. "You can decline dinner invitations you do not wish to accept, that sort of thing."

"Ladies," Gilbert said in a low voice, his eyes never leaving

Joy's for a moment, "are generally considered safer with widowers. Have you noticed that, Joy Fitzroy?"

Joy swallowed. Well, he clearly had the same sort of things on his mind, even if she had not said them. Gilbert appeared to know precisely what she wanted, what she craved, what she could not ask for—and now he was giving her a chance to ask for them.

The question was: was she brave enough, now she had been given an opening, to ask?

"And…and am I safe with you?"

Joy did not look away from Gilbert as she spoke, and she saw a flash of something dark and delicious spark in his eyes.

His hand resting on the back of the sofa moved, ever so slightly. His fingers curled, gently brushing the nape of her neck, and Joy gasped at the intense intimacy as shivers of delight rushed down her spine.

"Gilbert…" she breathed.

He grinned wickedly. "I do not think you are safe with me, no."

His movement was swift. Before Joy could say anything—not that she would have protested—Gilbert had covered the distance between them on the sofa, pulled her into his arms, and placed a passionate kiss upon her lips.

And not just passionate: eager. Determined. Joy could taste his desire, a flavor she was starting to crave with each and every kiss they shared, and she responded just as eagerly, clutching his cravat to pull him closer, closer, though she could not have him close enough.

His tongue teased open her lips as shivers of pleasure washed through her, and Joy moaned, craving more, growing bolder in her ardor as her tongue met his—first hesitantly, then boldly, demanding more and more from him until Gilbert broke apart from her, panting slightly, gazing into her eyes.

"Damn, Joy, whenever I think I know you, you end up surprising me."

Joy smiled weakly. "Surprise me? I consider myself surprised at every moment of our... Gilbert, you...you make me—"

"I know," interrupted Gilbert, "and I want it too."

She blinked. She had not actually said the words, had not known how to untangle them from around her tongue, but Gilbert had known, hadn't he? Perhaps he'd tasted it in her, seen it in her eyes, divined it from the eager way her fingertips had already scrabbled to untie his cravat.

She wanted him. Wanted all of him, everything he could give her. Lovemaking, bedding, whatever one wanted to call it, she wanted it, and from him.

She craved him. She cared for him deeply. He was a good man, a fine conversationalist, and he awoke in her something she had never felt.

Joy had laughed at the few ladies of her general acquaintance who claimed to fall instantly in love with their husbands. Justification, she had always considered it, for a rushed marriage or a marriage of alliance. But now...

Well. She would not call it love. Not aloud. But what else could it be?

"I have offended you."

"No—no!" Joy said hastily, seeing the look of concern on Gilbert's face. "No, it is just... Well, no other gentleman has ever—"

"I know," Gilbert interrupted, all eagerness and passion once again. "And I would not offer myself to you if I did not desire you most ardently, Joy. You have made me alive when I was dead, have awakened in me passions I have never felt...never."

Joy stared. *Never felt—not even with his wife?*

"Let me love you," Gilbert begged, a desperate tone in his voice. "I will not sleep until I have given you such pleasure as you have never known, Joy. I ache to give you that."

"And I want you too," Joy admitted, hardly aware how she was able to say such things but knowing she had to say them now, or never at all. "B-but I do not... I have never—"

Gilbert released her, and the pain of his absence was almost physical, Joy had craved it so. He rose from the sofa and stood before her, holding out his hand with a look on his face Joy had never seen.

"Let me show you," he said quietly. "Let me show you all the ways a man can love a woman. I will not say gentleman, for some of what I wish to share with you…'tis unrefined, yet no less the pleasurable. Let me show you, Joy."

Joy hesitated but for a moment. She was not about to walk away from such an offer—his silence and discretion hardly needed to be requested. She could trust him, she was sure.

And besides, in a few days he would be gone from Bath and from her life. No consequences, no possibility of discovery. All she had to do was give in to her urges.

Joy rose, took Gilbert's hand, and kissed it. "Show me."

A smile broke out on Gilbert's face: hungry, eager, grateful, myriad emotions that flashed by so quickly, Joy could not entirely make out all of them.

She did not need to. Thinking was no longer what she wanted to do. Thinking was something she did every day. This evening was not about thinking; it was about feeling. It was about losing herself in the glorious touches of a man who knew precisely what he was doing.

"Shall…shall we go upstairs?" she whispered, eyes flicking to the door.

When she looked back at Gilbert, it was to see a wicked smile.

"Why? What's wrong with right here?"

Joy's mouth fell open as she looked around the drawing room. To make love here, without a bed, where others would one day sit…he could not be serious!

"Oh, Joy, I have so much to teach you," said Gilbert, kissing her neck just under her ear. "So much…"

Joy's breathing quickened as his breath and lips moved down her neck. Prickles of delightful, sensual pleasure poured down her skin, and her heart beat frantically as Gilbert's hands moved to her waist, pulling her closer.

Heat was pooling between her legs, a desire, an ache she had glimpsed the last time Gilbert kissed her, but it was eager now, more insistent.

Giving in to the decadence of the moment, Joy clutched at Gilbert, pulling his head up to kiss his lips. She had never been so bold, so direct, but with Gilbert she knew she was safe.

At least, safe from judgment. Joy had never felt more on the edge of a precipice.

"May I remove your gown?"

Joy stared up into Gilbert's eyes as he broke the kiss and asked her that tantalizing question. *Remove her gown?* Of course, she knew it would be necessary, desirable even, but the thought of actually being naked before him…

There was a far-too-knowing smile on Gilbert's face. "I'll go first."

"What do you—"

But Joy did not have to ask any further—he made it perfectly clear. Stepping back only a pace from her, Gilbert did not take his eyes away as he hastily stripped, coat and waistcoat, cravat and shirt falling to the carpet in quick succession.

Joy swallowed. Gilbert was older than her, yes, but he had seemingly lost none of the strength of his youth. A broad chest covered in silver and black hair spread down toward his breeches, where his fingers were even now fumbling.

"Gilbert—"

She was not entirely sure what she would have said if her throat had permitted her to continue, but it was impossible. Gilbert had pulled off both boots and breeches and stood before her, in his own drawing room, utterly naked.

Joy stared.

Well, it was impossible not to. Here was a man, fully a man, every inch of him exuding power and desire and something indescribable, and she could not help but step forward and place a hand on his chest.

Gilbert's skin was warm, and his heart was beating frantical-ly—perhaps as frantically as her own. For some reason, it gave Joy courage. He was just as intrigued, as excited, as aroused as she was. And speaking of arousal…

"You can touch me," Gilbert breathed, "if you want to."

Joy did not have to ask what part of Gilbert he meant. It was difficult to ignore. His manhood stood erect, a dark pink, clearly aching to be touched. For her touch.

Hesitating only for a moment, Joy reached out a hand and stroked Gilbert's manhood. It throbbed, twitching slightly, and a moan escaped his mouth, giving Joy greater confidence. Oh, to make him utter that sound again, to give him pleasure as he had given her pleasure…

Joy was not sure what made her do it. An instinct, perhaps, something deep within her that told her precisely what to do.

She let go of his manhood and felt Gilbert's disappointment radiate off his body. Joy moved her fingers to the ties of her gown and heard his breathing quicken. She felt glorified in the way that just a suggestion of her body affected him.

Her own breathing hitched slightly as Joy allowed her gown to fall to the floor, and with it her underclothes and stays.

The drawing room was cold; that surely had to be the reason why Joy's skin was shivering, quivering.

Gilbert's eyes were wide and he reached out a hand. "Joy—"

"No." Joy had not intended to speak so severely, but she knew she would be utterly overcome if he touched her now.

If she was going to do what she wanted, taste what she want-ed, he would have to wait.

Gilbert immediately dropped his hand to his side. "I will not do anything you do not wish me to—"

"And neither will I," Joy said with a nervous smile. "So you must tell me if you want me to stop."

A flash of confusion covered his face—until Joy very slowly, without tearing her gaze away from Gilbert's, lowered herself to her knees.

His eyes darkened. "Joy, you don't know what you're—"

"You're right, I don't," said Joy quietly, inching forward, still gazing into his eyes. "And I want to explore. You don't mind if I explore, do you, Gilbert?"

He groaned as she reached out and touched his hips. "God, no."

Joy looked directly at the manhood before her. It looked larger from here, just as eager for her, just as hungry. And the desire to know what it tasted like, to know how it would feel in her mouth, to lick his skin and know him better, overcame her.

Gently, she moved a hand to guide it into her mouth.

"Oh, Joy!"

Gilbert bunched his fingers in her hair, disturbing pins and allowing some of it to fall down to her shoulders, but Joy was not concentrating on that. She was more focused on the warm, throbbing flesh within her mouth, twisting her tongue around it and glorying in the way Gilbert twitched with every movement.

Slowly, slowly, she eased his manhood from her mouth and licked the end. "You taste...you taste good."

Gilbert moaned. "Joy, you don't have to—"

"I know I don't have to," said Joy quietly, glancing up and seeing genuine pleasure painted across his face. "But I want to."

She did not give him any time to say anything more. Easing his manhood back into her mouth, Joy sucked ever so slightly and heard Gilbert moan, felt the tension increase in his fingers in her hair, and knew there was a way she could bring him pleasure that she had never expected.

It started gradually. Nipping her lips along his breadth, gripping his hips to keep him steady, Joy explored him, licking the length of him, learning what made Gilbert shudder and what made him cry out, and soon she was sucking, moving him in and out of her mouth, adoring his twitches, the way he moaned her name.

Oh, to hear Gilbert Kitteridge moan her name every day

would be a delight indeed.

"Joy—Joy, I want—Oh, yes," groaned Gilbert, putting a little pressure on her head to show her the rhythm he wanted.

Joy obeyed, delighting in the seamless understanding flowing between them, and feeling something pool between her own legs, a desire to be kissed this way, though she could of course not ask for such a thing, and then suddenly—

"Joy!" Gilbert cried.

He thrust violently into her mouth, once, twice, three times, and something hot and wet and salty poured into her mouth, and Joy swallowed again and again, absorbing it all and taking it all, his gift to her, his proof that she had kissed him to within an inch of his life.

Gilbert pulled himself from her mouth and fell backward onto the sofa, panting hard.

Joy wiped her mouth with the back of her hand and looked up eagerly, unsure now what to do or say. "Gilbert…"

He was panting hard still, breath caught in his lungs, but smiled as he looked wearily at her. "Damn, woman," he managed. "Ladies like you are not supposed to know things like that."

Joy smiled nervously. "I-I didn't. I just…wanted to know how you tasted."

Gilbert closed his eyes for a moment as though gathering strength, then looked fiercely at her. "And I could say the same."

Before she knew it, Gilbert had launched himself from the sofa and barreled her over. Their laughter mingled as he pushed Joy onto her back right before the dying embers of the fire.

"Remember, Joy, any time you want me to stop," Gilbert said softly as he kissed the corner of her mouth, "just say."

Joy was about to ask what on earth he meant, but she was unable to say a word as her back arched and her body quivered at the intensity of the sensations between her legs.

Her unspoken, silent wish had been answered. Gilbert was—was kissing her. There. Between her legs.

And not just kissing. Panting, Joy managed to prop herself up on her elbows to see Gilbert kneeling between her legs, his mouth affixed to her secret place, his tongue within her, and she could barely breathe, but breath was not needed…not when such ecstasies were being explored together.

"Oh, don't stop," she said.

Quite to the contrary, Gilbert lifted his head. "What are you—Why are you looking?"

Joy met his eyes and knew she could speak the truth. "Because I want to watch."

He shook his head. "Joy Fitzroy, you are everything I want in a woman."

"And you are everything I want in a man, but one thing."

He looked concerned at that, and Joy smiled.

"You aren't kissing me," she pointed out, heart racing, knowing she would never be this open with anyone ever again. "There. Now."

"I'll do whatever you want."

He did not waste any more time on words, and for that Joy was intensely thankful. He returned to her secret place, licking and kissing, twisting pleasure that rippled through her body, causing her to arch her back again—and then he lifted a hand from her hips where he had been keeping her steady, and grabbed her breast.

"Gilbert!"

Joy did not understand why such a touch elevated her pleasure to such a degree, but it did. His tongue within her, his fingers twisting and teasing her nipple—she could no longer support herself on her elbows and see the erotic sight of him pleasuring her, but she did not need to.

The ache within her was building, building, and Joy's eyelashes fluttered shut as she lost herself to the wave that was threatening to break at any moment.

Any moment—

"Gilbert!" Joy cried as her body burst apart with pleasure,

ecstasy and hedonistic agony showering her as her body rocked, her hips tightening to keep Gilbert's head in place as his tongue flickered across that delightful spot.

And then it was over.

Joy tried to open her eyes. Stars appeared on the ceiling of the drawing room as she tried to get back her breathing. And that was pleasure? That was lovemaking? It was a miracle anyone got anything done, with such delights to share.

Gilbert appeared above her, his legs nestled between hers. "Joy?"

She smiled weakly. "Do we get to do that again—Gilbert!"

His manhood had slid into her; she was slick and wet from his tongue, and already curls of pleasure were starting to mount through her body.

He grinned. "Again? Again, and again, and again…"

CHAPTER NINE

WHEN JOY OPENED her eyes, it was to see to her relief that the wondrous images she had in her mind were not a dream, but memories.

They had to be. There was no other explanation for her being here, in Gilbert Kitteridge's home, his drawing room, lying beside him on the floor in the early hours of the morning…utterly naked.

A small smile crept across her face. Well, she had done it. Something she had never thought she ever would. Lovemaking, pleasure, the way a person could kiss another into oblivion, and she had shared it all with a gentleman whose face was as dear to her as her own.

Gilbert slept on the floor beside her, utterly lost to the world.

They had pulled many blankets and rugs together and made a sort of nest, where delight after delight had been taken. The heat of their passion had kept them warm, and even now Joy could feel flushes of heat soaring through her body at the mere memory of what they had shared.

"Do we get to do that again—Gilbert!"

"Again? Again, and again, and again…"

She shivered, not from cold but from astonishment that she had permitted herself to do such a thing, share such a thing, be such a woman.

It was not the sort of thing a lady did, let alone a Fitzroy. Oh, the scandal it would cause if anyone knew precisely what Miss Fitzroy had done with Mr. Kitteridge that evening!

But Joy knew it would stay between them. There was no reason to share such information with others, and besides, he would be leaving soon. Gilbert would disappear from Bath and her life, and she would have to learn to live without him.

Her heart twisted painfully at the thought. A Bath without Gilbert—a life without him.

How was she ever to survive?

Gilbert twitched in his sleep, turning so he faced not her but the empty fireplace.

Joy bit her lip. She was not one for goodbyes, never had been. It was painful to see a part of one's life disappear; to say goodbye was to acknowledge the end of that moment.

No, far better to creep away, find her gown and dress as silently as she could manage in the hall—thank the Lord there were no servants about—and leave Gilbert to slumber. It would only be more difficult to face him, to accept what they had shared could never be repeated, to admit there was no possibility of a future together.

For a moment, Joy tried to imagine what such a future could be. The two of them—no, the four of them; she could not forget the two turtle doves—living in a big old house in the country.

Joy tried as best she could, as her skin started to cool and the memories of the evening before faded, but it was no use.

She had lived her entire life with her parents in the city of Bath. A country life was something that happened to other people—and as for caring for someone else's daughters…

Joy swallowed. She would not know where to start.

No, it was better it ended this way, with all the memories and moments of pleasure, than attempt something that simply would not work. Besides, Joy was certain she had no desire to be the fairytale stepmother so many feared or hated.

She would take her memories of herself and Gilbert ravishing each other, seeing who could make the other come with pleasure first, and lock them away in her heart and take them out to examine on special occasions.

Something never to be repeated.

Slowly, Joy edged out of the nest she and Gilbert had built without disturbing him. He slept soundly on, as though she was not there.

In a way, she supposed darkly, she wasn't.

The hall was freezing, and she swiftly pulled on both under-clothes and gown, shivering slightly. Her stays were completely impossible to do alone, and that provided her with a rather difficult challenge.

Well, it was not as though she could walk through Bath with her stays in her hands!

Joy almost laughed at the image, but managed to control herself. She did not wish to wake Gilbert—she did not want any awkward questions or a certainly awkward leave taking.

So what was she to do?

Swallowing hard, Joy knew there was only one thing to do. Go to Harmony's, attempt to hide her stays in her pelisse, so her sister would have no opportunity to guess at what had occurred, and ask to borrow their carriage.

It would not be too difficult, surely, to convince Harmony into helping her. Her sister never asked too many questions, anyway.

Joy closed Gilbert's front door as quietly as she could manage, wincing slightly at the clatter of the knocker, and quickly stepped down his path and up her sister's. The air was freezing. It was, after all, just a few days until Christmas Eve, and snow still lined the ground.

A quick pull of Harmony's bell. A maid opened the door with a look of astonishment.

"Miss Fitzroy! What—"

"Yes, yes, it is early, you did not expect me," said Joy in a rush, shivering in the cold. "Move aside, there's a dear."

Even just a minute outside had chilled her to the bone, and Joy was certain there was no possibility of her walking home with her stays wrapped in her pelisse. Not at this hour, not without causing scandal if she was seen by someone of the *ton*. No, she had made the right decision by coming to her sister—even though, Joy found as she stepped into the morning room, she had evidently surprised her.

"Joy Fitzroy, what on earth," began Harmony, startled up from her seat where she was reading, Rufus playing at her feet. "What happened?"

Joy opened her mouth, and then closed it again.

Ah. Yes. So focused had she been on hiding her stays and making sure she could ask her sister for the use of her carriage, she had not actually concocted an idea to explain why she had turned up at her sister's door in the early morning, needing a carriage. *Blast.*

"Morning, Harmony," Joy said with a weak smile, as though that would distract her from the rather startling sight of her sister at such an odd time. "And how are you?"

"Very well, I think—but what are you doing here?" asked Harmony, evidently not willing to be so easily distracted. "And your hair is so wild!"

Joy raised a hand to her hair and realized, quite to her surprise, that it was entirely loose, flowing down her shoulders.

Well, of course it was. The antics she and Gilbert had enjoyed earlier had not been conducive to keeping her hair in pins.

A soft smile crept across her face, then Joy pushed it aside. No, there was absolutely no chance of her revealing all to her sister. She would simply think of an excuse.

A believable excuse.

If only one came to mind…

"Joy, it is near seven o'clock in the morning," said Harmony, still staring at her sister. "I am only awake because Rufus had a nightmare and so we came here to… What happened to you? I thought Mr. Kitteridge was taking you home in his carriage?"

Joy swallowed. Yes, that was what they had said, and it had felt all good and proper at the time…but she was glad indeed that the night had taken a different turn.

Not that she could say anything like this to Harmony.

Something strange flickered across her sister's face, and she bent down to speak to her son. "Rufus, go on upstairs and wake your father. It's high time he was up. Stay with him and make sure he does, will you?"

The toddler giggled at the idea of telling his father what to do—at least, that was what Joy assumed—and ran out of the room, slamming the door behind him.

Harmony winced. "It does not matter how many times I say… Joy. Sit here."

She pointed imperiously at the chair opposite her, and for some reason, Joy felt as though she had no choice but to obey. Perhaps it was the mother in Harmony, now she had a child. Whatever it was, there was no opportunity to say no.

Joy stepped across the room, sat down heavily in the chair, and placed her pelisse—with stays wrapped inside—on her lap.

Well, what's Harmony going to say now? she thought wearily. Would she chastise her sister for being here so early, or ask whether something was wrong with their parents—perhaps she would assume Joy had come to bring a message about one of their cousins.

It would not be about her, of that Joy was certain.

So it was with an impressive amount of calm that her sister said, "Did you stay the night with Mr. Kitteridge?"

"Stay—stay the night?" Joy spluttered, eyes wide. How to goodness had she known that? "Certainly not! I would never— Stay the night! That you could suggest such a thing!"

The normally shy Harmony, however, did not look away, nor look ashamed at the question. "I am not suggesting such a thing, but everything about you is. Look at your hair, Joy—your flushed cheeks! You are not wearing stays, I can tell by the hang of your gown, and you look…different."

Joy flushed, dropping her gaze to her pelisse. It was impossible; Harmony simply could not tell by looking at her!

But then, she was the sister with more experience in this area—even Joy had to admit it. Harmony had been married nigh on six years now, and surely knew the signs, knew what to look for.

"You… He made love to you, didn't he?"

Joy swallowed. Then she nodded.

Though words had utterly failed her, the rush of embarrassment she had expected did not come. It was most unaccountable; if she had admitted to anyone else that her innocence was gone, with someone her family knew, Joy had assumed she would be overcome with a desire to disappear instantly.

But that was not the case. No, quite to the contrary, in a way Joy was…proud of it. Proud to have been chosen by Gilbert, proud to have been desired by him.

"Joy Fitzroy, I never would have believed it of you," said Harmony.

Joy smiled wryly as she looked up and saw no judgment, but much surprise on her sister's face. "I am not sure I can believe it of myself."

The two sisters laughed together for a moment, and Joy felt a rush of relief at having spoken the words aloud. It made it all the more real, somehow, as nothing else had.

"But it will never happen again."

Harmony frowned. "You think not?"

Joy swallowed. How could her sister ask? A meaningful connection with Gilbert would be…complicated, to put it mildly. A widower, a father of two daughters, a gentleman who did not live in Bath…and they hardly knew each other. It was madness to think this glorious emotion she felt toward him was love.

Wasn't it?

"Joy," Harmony began softly, "I really think—"

"How very rude of you to send our son to—Oh. Hullo, Joy," said David from the door.

Joy jolted round to look at her brother-in-law, who was smiling awkwardly as he looked at his wife for direction.

"I do apologize, but I needed you up," said Harmony smoothly. "Where is he?"

"In the kitchen, irritating Cook," David said as he shut the door behind him. "She loves him so much that I hadn't the heart to remove him. Joy, is everything quite well?"

Joy realized for a second time what a bedraggled mess she must look—her gown imperfectly tied, her hair loose, falling past her shoulders. The concern in her brother-in-law's eyes was intense; he clearly believed something awful had happened to her.

When it was quite the opposite.

"David," she said, taking a deep breath, "last night I lost my innocence to Gilbert Kitteridge."

The reactions from the married couple were impressive and distinct.

Harmony's mouth fell open, a gasp escaping her throat as she rose to her feet. "Joy!"

But David was quite different. Joy saw to her astonishment that he clenched his fists, his jaw tightening as a nerve pulsed in his throat. "Willingly?"

It took Joy a moment to understand what her brother-in-law was saying, and once she did, a wave of affection for the man who had truly become her brother washed over her.

"Very willingly, I am afraid," Joy said dryly. "You have nothing to fear there. He did not force himself on me."

Quite the opposite, she wanted to say, but she was not sure her sister would cope with such information.

David encouraged his wife to sit before standing behind her. "Well."

"Well indeed!" said Harmony breathlessly, still staring at her sister. "Joy, I cannot believe you said that to my husband!"

"Why not?" Joy shrugged. "I have known him for six years; he should know me well enough by now."

A low chuckle came from her brother-in-law. "I do indeed,"

said David. "Well. My word."

"My word," echoed his wife.

Joy sat awkwardly, unsure whether she was being reprimanded. It was ridiculous, really—Harmony was years younger than her. A younger sister should not reprimand the elder.

But then, she had done precisely what was forbidden within Society. Losing her innocence to a man like that—even a widower, despite her bold words just days ago to their mother—was not something that was ever done. If the truth were ever to be known...

"And do you care for Mr. Kitteridge?"

David's question was one Joy should have been expecting, but to her surprise, she found she had no answer.

"I...I think so," she said, not quite willing yet to delve into the deeper parts of herself to discover the answer.

Care for Mr. Kitteridge—for Gilbert?

Of course she cared for him. "Care" did not fully encompass her heart. A great deal of emotion was tangled up with him now, and not merely because they had exchanged such sweet pleasures...pleasures Joy wished, though she knew it was impossible, to share again.

But there was a whole part of his life that she did not know, could not know. His daughters, his life in the countryside, his late wife...

All of that was strange to her, and Joy knew it would take a great deal for him to share it with her. She was not unwilling, not in the slightest, but it was for Gilbert to decide whether to share such intimacies with her.

"You think so?" repeated Harmony.

Her husband shook his head. "You need to know, Joy. You have to be certain, absolutely certain, that he is someone you cannot spend your life without."

Joy swallowed. The way he spoke: so simply, so calmly. With no concern or embarrassment at all. "How did you know?"

Harmony looked up at her husband with a sickly-sweet smile, and David looked at her with the same expression.

"Love at first sight," he murmured.

"Perhaps even earlier," said Harmony. "You know, we think it most likely I heard David and his eleven pipers before we ever actually met, and I am sure the way he played his music…"

Joy nodded, ignoring the minutiae of her sister's words as she let them just wash over her. The general intent was clear enough.

"—and before we knew it, living without each other was impossible, and—"

Joy cleared her throat meaningfully.

Harmony looked away from her husband with a slight flush on her cheeks, as though she had momentarily forgotten her sister was there. "Look, this is not something you can just ignore."

"Certainly not," said David.

Joy's stomach lurched. "I cannot? Gilbert—Mr. Kitteridge is leaving Bath very soon. It is entirely possible I will not see him again, ever, or at least until next Season."

"If I were you, I would consider whether your affections for him are sufficient to wish for a more permanent understanding," said Harmony gently. "Matrimony, even."

Joy's eyes widened. Was not her sister advancing a little quickly in her thinking? Why, she had never met the man a week ago!

Yet her heart leapt at the mention of that word she had studiously attempted to ignore.

Matrimony.

Being Gilbert's wife. Being the mother to those two little turtle doves, seeing them grow—perhaps giving them siblings. Would that not be wonderful?

"And I would consider quickly," said Harmony, her voice still gentle. "Very quickly."

Joy's gaze sharpened as she looked inquisitively at her sister. "Really? Why?"

"Because," Harmony said with a wry smile, "he is standing behind you."

CHAPTER TEN

HEART IN HER mouth, hardly knowing how she was still able to breathe, Joy very slowly turned around in her seat.

There stood Gilbert Kitteridge. In the doorway. His eyes fixed on hers.

Joy swallowed, heart thumping wildly, all thought of attempting to explain herself, speaking at all, utterly flying from her mind.

For what could she say? She had revealed their intimacy to her sister, and now David, her brother-in-law, would expect Gilbert to—What would happen if he did not? Would it come to blows?

Joy's stomach lurched. Would they duel?

No, that was preposterous, she tried to tell herself. Gentlemen did not have duels, not anymore!

Not in public. But she had heard whispers; all Society had. Duels over a lady's honor that were settled privately, outside of Bath or London, or any reputable place. Duels fought to decide the honor of a lady.

A lady like her.

"Mr. Kitteridge," said David.

Joy twisted to look at her brother-in-law, heart painful in her chest. Did he own a pair of pistols? Surely not. David Navarre was a musician, a kind man, a gentle man…but there was nothing gentle in the way he was looking at Gilbert.

"I believe," said Harmony delicately, rising to her feet, "these two have plenty to talk about, and would best complete that conversation without our presence. Come on, David."

"But—"

"Come on," Harmony said firmly.

Joy almost laughed at the way her sister took David's hand and led him out of the room. Harmony was a gentle soul, a quiet, shy woman, really, but there was something about her when she had made up her mind.

That was when all the Fitzroy determination came through. It was in there, somewhere.

Joy would hate to get on the wrong side of her.

"No, wait," Joy said, suddenly realizing what was about to happen. "I am sure there is nothing Gilbert—Mr. Kitteridge and I cannot say to each other without you and—"

"We will see you later, Joy," Harmony said pointedly as she closed the door behind her, leaving Joy and Gilbert alone in the morning room.

Joy swallowed. Where was one supposed to look when faced with a gentleman who had been entirely naked the last time you had seen him?

"What are you—Why are you looking?"

"Because I want to watch."

Oh, such heady memories were quick to soar back into her mind, but it was ridiculous, of course. She could not allow herself to be so easily distracted, not when she had Gilbert right before her, looking…looking…

Joy was not sure what he looked like. There was a strange expression on his face as Gilbert stepped forward, quickly closing the gap between them.

Though unsure precisely why she did it, Joy rose to her feet. Perhaps she felt less vulnerable, attempting to meet Gilbert on the same level. Seated, she felt overwhelmed by him; his masculine presence already filled the room, making it difficult to think.

"Well, I think your sister is quite right," he said.

Joy blinked. "You...you do?"

She could hardly remember what her sister had said, now Gilbert was before her. Just a few feet away, almost the same distance they had been when she first removed her clothes...

"I do," said Gilbert. "Consider whether your affections for me are sufficient for more, I believe she said. I think, indeed, it is time for you to decide."

Joy stared. *Decide?* She did not even know what she was deciding between, had not comprehended there was a choice before her. What was she trying to decide? To be his mistress? To be his wife?

Until Gilbert offered her something, was it not his responsibility to make it clear precisely what she wanted?

It was difficult to look into the eyes of a man she had shared so much with, in the cold light of day, but Joy persevered and saw something rather strange in his eyes.

Was that...fear? Was it possible that Gilbert was just as afraid as she was?

"You ask me to decide, but I have no idea what you want me to decide between," Joy said helplessly, deciding complete honesty would be better than any other approach. "What do you want from me, Gilbert? What can you... Do you wish to offer me anything?"

There was surely a better way to ask that, but Joy was not sure what it was. How could she encapsulate in just a few words all her fears, all her worries, all her desires—the confusion that finding such a connection had brought, the fear she would never find such a thing again?

"You need to ask that?" said Gilbert. "Joy, I want you."

Joy shivered, hardly aware how such a phrase should be taken. He wanted her? Wanted her...to what? Wanted her to accept his lovemaking, but nothing more? Wanted her to be available to him whenever he came into town, but never build anything stronger than that?

Gilbert sighed with a slow laugh. "I can see in your eyes I have not made myself clear. Joy, I want you. I…I love you."

He *loved* her? Joy knew it was impossible, knew he was perhaps just saying these things to placate her, make her feel better about handing over her innocence less than twelve hours ago…

But a part of her rose, thrilled, at the admission.

Of course he loved her. Did not she love him? Had they not found something special, something precious—something that translated into such heat and such power when unclothed and kissing each other—that could never be repeated with any other?

"You love me?" Joy breathed.

If only she was bold enough to step forward and curl into his embrace, to feel his words, not just hear them—but Joy knew she had to concentrate, had to attempt as best she could to be in the moment.

This was a conversation she did not wish to rush.

"Love sounds strange when spoken to someone so new," Gilbert said, a smile dancing on his lips, "but there is no other word for how I feel about you, Joy. Obsession, desire, craving your very presence, yes, but it goes beyond that. Beyond anything I have ever felt."

Joy dropped her gaze slightly. She would not think it, would not even wonder—

"More than your wife?"

Gilbert's smile faltered.

Joy swallowed, knowing she should not have said such a thing, but also knowing she would have regretted it for the rest of her life if she had not. She had to know.

"My wife and I entered into an arranged marriage," said Gilbert quietly. "I married her the second occasion I met her, and she was dead within a year. I admit, I barely knew her. She was not one to share herself, but you… Joy, you are so different. Beautiful, as she was, but different. More open, more vulnerable, more willing to share of yourself. More sarcastic, too."

Joy had to laugh. "I do not suppose there is anyone more sarcastic than me."

"I have no wish to discover one," said Gilbert with a wry chuckle. "Because you, to me...you are perfection, Joy. You think I expected to find love, true love, a real love, more than anything I ever felt before, with a woman whom I met in Sydney Gardens?"

Joy's mind returned to that moment, that heady moment, just a few days ago, when she had sat on a freezing bench thinking about her lack of romance, her lack of family, her lack of a child...and a child had just fallen into her lap.

"I suppose I just need a family to fall into my lap this Christmas. Then I would fit in with the rest of the Fitzroys."

Her heart skipped a beat. "You love me."

Gilbert took her hands in his own, and Joy felt a surge of pleasure. This was where she belonged. "I love you, Joy, yes. I love what I know about you already, and I...I want to learn more. I want to know all of you. I...I want to marry you."

Joy's eyes widened as her fingers tightened around his. "You what?"

"I said I want to marry you," said Gilbert. "I want to spend my days laughing with you and my nights bedding you."

Joy flushed, though this time she did not look away. "I would like that, too."

The admission was one willingly made, even more so when she saw what happiness it gave the man she loved. Gilbert stepped forward as though to kiss her, but Joy put up a hand to stop him.

Gilbert stilled immediately. "What is it?"

Joy took a deep breath. She had to say it, even if it would end the romantic path they were on. "What about your daughters?"

He frowned. "What about them?"

It was difficult not to think of Jemima—both of them, Joy thought wryly. The little girl who played so happily with her twin sister, and the Jemima in Joy's life, Jemima Rotherham, who had once been Jemima Fitzroy. Her cousin, beloved by the family even though she was prickly, who had struggled so long with a stepmother of her own.

What if Jemima Kitteridge felt just the same? What if she and Paloma fought against the introduction of a mother in their lives, a mother, moreover, who had never met their own?

Was she about to condemn those two girls to a lifetime of misery?

Joy swallowed. Not that she could explain any of that coherently.

"Your daughters may not wish you to marry again," she said instead, holding on to his fingers tightly, as though that would keep him there forever. "They might be unhappy if…if we…"

She could not finish the sentence, but could see Gilbert understood.

"My two turtle doves want me to be happy," said Gilbert slowly. "They know of no other mother—in truth, they have been requesting one for some time. I can think of no one better."

Joy smiled at the praise, felt the warmth of it in her heart. She edged toward him, desperate to be closer.

Closer to Gilbert. The man she would…marry?

It all felt like a dream, it was happening so suddenly, though she had certainly heard of swifter matches. And besides, did they not know how compatible they were? Had they not conversed extensively about all manner of topics? Had they not tasted each other's delights? Did they not know how wonderful their coupling was?

"I want to be happy," Gilbert murmured, releasing one of her hands to cup her cheek. "For so long I have been alone, and you…you complete me, Joy."

Joy's heart leapt. "You're only saying that after I kissed and touched you…there."

In the light of Harmony's morning room, that was all she could manage to say, but Gilbert understood her well enough.

A twinkle glistened in his eye. "Well, I would be lying if I said

I had no wish for a repeat of last night, but Joy, you must know it is more than that. I want to be happy, and I want you to be happy."

"I want you to be happy too," Joy said.

Gilbert smiled. "I think you are the only one who can do that. So, will you? Will you marry me?"

Joy's head swam. It was all happening so quickly, so beyond her control, but then, had she not been waiting all her life for such a moment? Why wait any longer?

"I will," she breathed.

Gilbert crushed her into his embrace, claiming her lips just as he had claimed her last night. Joy reveled in his passion, giving herself up to him and eagerly parting her lips. A sigh escaped her as his kisses started to grow the aching need within her.

"I have half a mind to push you up against this wall and make you cry for mercy," Gilbert said as he kissed down her neck.

Joy shivered. "I'm of half a mind to let you."

Gilbert straightened up, eyes wide. "Joy Fitzroy, you wanton woman!"

"I want you," said Joy, laughing, "and there is plenty of time for that, but first…"

His smile broadened. "First?"

Joy grinned to see his eagerness. What it was to be desired, to be so hungry for someone who wanted you in just the same way. They would have a lifetime of exploration to enjoy, but before all of that…

"First we need to tell Harmony and David."

Gilbert groaned. "Can't it wait?"

"No," said Joy. "Because they are outside the house at the window, looking in."

Releasing her as though she had scalded him, Gilbert peered out of the window into the snowy street. Joy giggled as her sister and brother-in-law swiftly turned around and pretended not to see them.

"Well, I suppose I shall have to make an honest woman of

you now," Gilbert teased.

Joy took his hand in hers, intertwining her fingers with his. "We'll have to arrange the wedding for the turtle doves to join in—perhaps as flower girls?"

"You can have the wedding however you want," said Gilbert with a sigh before pulling her into his side and kissing the side of her head. "All I ask is that I am put in charge of one thing."

Joy looked up at him. "And that is…?"

Gilbert grinned, a wicked look once more in his eye. "The wedding night, of course."

About Emily E K Murdoch

If you love falling in love, then you've come to the right place.

I am a historian and writer and have a varied career to date: from examining medieval manuscripts to designing museum exhibitions, to working as a researcher for the BBC to working for the National Trust.

My books range from England 1050 to Texas 1848, and I can't wait for you to fall in love with my heroes and heroines!

Follow me on twitter and instagram @emilyekmurdoch, find me on facebook at facebook.com/theemilyekmurdoch, and read my blog at www.emilyekmurdoch.com.